Flesh Communion

and Other Stories

Holly Rae Garcia

EASTON FALLS PUBLISHING

For Ryan

Contents

Regulators

She didn't see him watching her. They never did. He stood in the Action section of Fred's Video, running his hands along the tops of the VHS cases. The sharp plastic edge of a cracked cover snagged at his finger, pricking small drops of blood from it, but he didn't notice. He continued down the aisle as she moved, his hand still touching the movies, leaving pink smudges along the tops as he went. She was just a few rows over, trying to decide between *Pulp Fiction* or *The Shawshank Redemption*. Her head bobbed to the music piping through the speakers in the ceiling. Her name was Tiffany, and she was perfect. Blue jean overalls hugged her curves. The left strap was undone, exposing the almost-sheer white crop top beneath. *Tiffany*. He whispered her name to himself, shuddering at the way it rolled across his tongue. She bit the bottom edge of her lip, in the way that she did when she concentrated. He knew this because he had watched her, there at that store every Saturday night for the past month, like clockwork.

She made her decision. As she swung around to place the rejected movie back in its slot, her blond ponytail bobbed into view over the top of the stacks. The yellow scrunchie holding it all together had seen better days, but he didn't mind that. She was young, but not too young. He wasn't a monster, after all. He'd known a few guys that liked 'em younger, but they were disgusting, vile creatures. Not him. He was all class and sophistication. You had to be smart when you played those games, and he hadn't been caught yet.

Emerging from between the stacks, she headed for the front of the store clutching her decision, an empty plastic case for *Pulp Fiction*. The girl behind the counter, a teenager who only got the job because she was banging the owner's nephew, put down the book she was reading and greeted her.

"Sup, Tiff?"

"Not much, just hanging out with this," she gestured to the movie case, "and Oliver. Same old boring Saturday night."

The girl nodded, sifting through the boxes below the counter before emerging with the tape. "Here you go. That's $3.26."

The teenager didn't notice the man, who was watching the woman (who also didn't notice him.) No one ever saw him, not the women he hunted, not the bystanders who could identify him later, not a single person. And he liked it that way. You could get away with an awful lot when you were invisible.

But invisibility would only get you so far. To have fun, the *real* kind of fun that he longed for, he had to show himself eventually, and the time had come. He had watched her long enough. Her habits, her smell, her intoxicating smile, he knew it all by then. He shuffled down the aisle toward the front counter, and the small bell above the door jingled as the woman walked through to the parking lot.

"You're bleeding!"

Tearing his eyes away from the back of Tiffany's head, he glanced at the girl behind the counter. "What?"

"*Hello*, you're bleeding. Your hand is bleeding."

In the time it took him to look down at his hand and back up through the large glass windows, Tiffany had climbed into her white sedan and shut the door. Ignoring his hand, he rushed outside, the bell an angry clang as he shoved the door open.

"You can't just bleed on everything, dickweed—"

He ignored her. Fuck it, let *her* clean up the mess. He wiped his hand on the side of his jeans and jumped into his 1984 Mercury Cougar, which he lovingly referred to as "The Silver Bullet." The thing was as big as a damn boat, but she ran good.

Most of the time.

The man watched Tiffany pull out of the parking lot, and then take a right on Spencer Avenue. Gunning his engine, he put The Silver Bullet in drive and followed her.

***

Tiffany turned onto Spencer and headed toward the highway. One of her headlights was out, so a single ray of light pierced the night ahead of her as she drove. She'd have to get that fixed, the last thing she needed was a cop pulling her over. Not that she had anything against the police, their interactions just always seemed to leave a bad taste in her mouth. Her movie rental sat on the passenger seat next to her, rattling around as she hit potholes and bumps in the road. She had been looking forward to seeing that movie ever since it came out. She had missed it in the theater over a shitty blind date. They were supposed to have a drink at the pub, then walk over to the movies. One drink turned into several, then turned into her date getting shit-faced before they could even make it out of the bar. That was the first and last time she let her friend, Jenny, fix her up with anyone. She didn't care how cute he was, or how much money he made.

She had excused herself to use the restroom and darted for the back door when he wasn't looking. She should have gone on by herself to see the movie but didn't want to risk running into him if he decided to head that way. Good riddance, anyway. She was just mad that she shaved her legs for him. Just in case, you know. A woman had to be prepared for every possible outcome. And it had been a long while since Tiffany had seen *that* particular...outcome.

Renting was better, anyway. Tiffany spent many nights in her pajamas, curled up on the couch, a movie popped into the VCR and her cat, Oliver, on her lap. Not a bad life at all, she figured.

She was singing along to "Regulate" by Warren G when she felt her right hip vibrating. Tiffany turned the volume dial down, and a shrill beeping filled the car. She grabbed the wheel with her left hand and wrestled the pager off her hip and out from under her seatbelt with her right.

"07734," pager-speak for "Hello."

She tossed the pager next to the VHS tape. Tiffany was running a tad behind schedule, and Jenny was eager to hear from her.

Neon lights flashed up ahead, signaling a skeezy hotel just off the road on the right. Tiffany flipped her blinker on, hoping the silver piece of shit riding her ass would notice. As if there weren't two whole other lanes he could have been in.

Gravel crunched beneath her tires as she aimed her car for the bank of payphones just outside the hotel's office. Red and Yellow bursts of light filtered down from the sign above, reflecting onto the metal phone booths like an electronic rave.

Behind her, the silver car edged into the parking lot.

***

He couldn't plan it better anymore if he tried. And those days, he barely had to try. Despite the "stranger danger" advertisements, women didn't really pay attention to their surroundings. Otherwise, he'd have a lot less fun on the nights he hunted.

The white sedan was parked up ahead, next to the payphones. He slowed The Silver Bullet to a crawl, inching closer to his prey. He finally rolled to a stop a few feet behind Tiffany's car as her door swung open and two denim-clad legs reached out to the gravel beneath. When she glanced back at him, he smiled. He knew he had a great smile. Women had always loved that about him, it was something that allowed him to disarm them immediately.

She smiled back, waved at him, then walked to one of the phone booths.

He chuckled to himself. That wave. That *smile.* Most women were so afraid of offending someone or being thought of as rude, that they just dropped their defenses at the first sign of friendliness. Because really, what was the other option? Ignore him? *Rude.*

Tiffany turned her back to him, picked up one of the phones, and started punching the silver squares on the number pad.

***

A car door opened and closed with twin thuds behind her. The man in the silver car had gotten out and was now walking toward the payphones. She supposed it was the casual wave that had emboldened him.

She held her breath, sensing him close. Cheap cologne wafted toward her—a gift, probably, from some Aunt who didn't know any better. Or worse, he bought it for himself. He probably thought it made him smell...*sexy*.

Tiffany rolled her eyes and cleared her throat.

"Hey, Jenny? Yeah, it's me. I'm ready when you are." She talked into the phone, gripping the handset so tight her knuckles paled.

"It's about damn time."

The man turned around and came face-to-face with a tall brunette woman. Behind him, Tiffany swung the handset around, ripping the cord from the booth, and slammed it into the back of the man's head. He crumpled to the ground.

"What took you so long? You were supposed to be here half an hour ago." The woman scowled at Tiffany as they dragged the man into the woods behind the hotel.

"I couldn't figure out what movie I wanted to rent, take a chill pill. We're here now, aren't we?" Tiffany grunted as she heaved the man onto a pile of leaves. "This was the easiest one yet." She wiped the sweat off her brow and looked at Jenny.

"He's not exactly a fine specimen, but I guess he'll do," Jenny shrugged.

"Well, I don't see *you* bringing anyone around!"

The man coughed as he came to, and his eyes searched the woods around him before landing on the women. He jumped to his feet, then staggered backward, grabbing his head in agony.

Jenny glared at her friend, "It takes all the fun out of it when you hit 'em that hard right away."

Tiffany kicked the man's legs out from under him and he fell to his knees, hands frantically searching in the leaves around him for something to use as a weapon against the women. They had seen that before, desperate men seemed to think they'll find a damn crowbar in the middle of the woods. Sometimes they came up with a stick, or a rock, or some other useless bit.

Jenny grabbed the man's arms and crouched down, holding his hands above his head while Tiffany straddled him.

"Is this what you thought you were gonna get tonight, cowboy? Huh? You like that?" Tiffany gyrated against him, pushing him further through the pile of leaves and into the soft ground below.

The man's scream was cut off when she leaned forward, covering his mouth with hers. They all liked to be kissed, at least once. Gave them a little something to go out with, anyway. Not the bang they were hoping for, but close enough.

Tiffany's mouth widened, and her upper lip covered his nose while her bottom stretched across his chin. She moaned, and each lip split in two. All four lips covered the man's entire face, groping and suckling as they went, leaving trails of blood across his cheeks. Her tongue peeked out, the tip covered with sharp barbs, and slithered over his face and around to the back of his neck. She was just getting started.

"Save some for me," Jenny grunted, still holding onto the man's arms.

Tiffany's eyes darted upwards at her friend, then back down to the man beneath her, struggling to breathe. He bucked his hips and kicked his legs, but he was no match for her. Tiffany pressed into him again, until the soft crack of bones echoed through the forest around them. His eyes flew open in pain, and he struggled to scream.

"Ok, my turn," Jenny pleaded.

Tiffany sighed and rolled off the man's broken pelvis, releasing his face from the grip of her mouth. He gasped for breath, breathed in deeply, then tried to scream again.

Jenny was on top of him before he could utter a sound, covering his face with her own painful kisses and pushing her hips against his broken bottom half.

Tiffany held his arms and leaned down, whispering in his ear, "You like that, big boy? How's it feel?" She sat back up, a trail of tendons and skin stretching from her mouth to the hole in the side of his head where his ear used to be. She closed her eyes as she chewed. She swallowed and took a deep breath.

"Why do the perverts always taste so yummy?"

Jenny mumbled around a mouthful of the man's cheek, chewed, then wiped her lips with the back of her hand before answering, "I think it's something about the adrenaline getting into the meat. They know better than anyone else, what's gonna happen to 'em. They've done it to others a hundred times. Well, maybe not *this* exactly..." She leaned down to his mouth and gripped his tongue with her teeth. The man squealed in agony.

"Hey, you got the tongue last time."

Jenny sat up, the man's tongue hanging from her mouth. She spit it toward her friend. "My bad, there you go."

"Jesus Christ, Jenny. Now you've gotten it all dirty," Tiffany complained as she pulled the meat from the dirt below her. She dusted it off with her hands, blew on it, and then popped it into her mouth with a smile.

The man tried to scream, but without a tongue and only half of his face remaining, nothing came out but a weak gurgle.

The women continued feasting as the moon shone down on them. Jenny, finally satiated, leaned against a tree and patted her swollen belly. A pile of bloody clothes was all that was left where the man used to be. Tiffany sucked the marrow from a vertebrae before she popped it into her mouth, crunching the bone into a fine powder and then swallowing. Her lips conformed back to human standards, and she licked her fingers and grinned.

Jenny pulled a pack of cigarettes from her back pocket, "Got a light?"

Tiffany dug through the man's jeans and tossed a blood-soaked lighter to Jenny.

She swiped her hand across the top, flickering blood into the air as the flame caught.

"Was it good for you?" Tiffany asked before taking a drag off Jenny's cigarette.

"Always," answered Jenny. "*Always*. But I get the tongue next time."

"Yeah, yeah. Hey, did you hear about the rapist over in Woodsbury?"

"Yeah...he only goes after coeds, right?"

"Yep."

"Looks like we're going to Woodsbury."

"After tonight, I won't be hungry again for a week, at least."

Jenny climbed to her feet, brushing leaves and dirt from her jeans. "Well, I'm gonna bounce."

"See you next time. You know the drill."

"I'll page you, try to stick to the schedule next time, could you? I don't wanna be waiting around all night again."

"You're so fucking dramatic." Tiffany waved to her friend as she disappeared into the woods.

Jenny never liked driving to their meetups, preferring instead to walk. She said it was how she kept her trim figure. Tiffany never really cared about her figure. As long as it pulled the men in, she figured she was doing all right. She leaned over to collect the man's clothes and headed back to her car by the payphones.

The night clerk at the hotel, a scruffy-haired kid in an Weezer T-shirt, stepped outside the office and stared at her. Tiffany knew what she must have looked like, covered in someone else's blood and carrying a pile of bloody clothing.

She smiled, tossed the man's keys to the clerk, and climbed into her car. By the time she pulled back onto the highway, the kid had pulled The Silver Bullet around to the back of the hotel. She never knew what he did with the cars. Didn't care, really. They had scratched each other's backs for years and would continue to do so as long as it was convenient for her.

Once home, she took a long hot shower and fed Oliver a few scraps she had snuck out in her pocket. He loved testicles the most and, while these were smaller than some of the others, he still purred in appreciation as he tore into them. By the time Tiffany had popped her movie into the VCR and sat down on the couch, the custom pizza oven in her kitchen roared with a golden glow, charring the man's belongings into an unrecognizable pile of ashes.

"Come here, Oliver."

The cat stopped cleaning himself, jumped up onto the couch, and nestled into her lap.

Not a bad Saturday night after all.

Flap

Claire pulled the tattered blanket closer and watched the window covering snatch a wayward bit of wind. The canvas whipped against the side of their tent in a slow dance, occasionally letting the two metal edges of the zipper kiss before pulling apart again.

Flap.

Ding.

Flap.

If the entire tent were made of zippers, then perhaps the resulting clamor would drown out the other sounds coming across the water from the mainland. The sounds the people made when they were running, the sounds they made when they were dying, and the deafening silence afterward that seemed loudest of all. The disease had taken over everything. Only their small island seemed safe, but time was running out. Claire pulled the blanket over her ears and focused on the window.

Flap.

Ding.

Flap.

From behind her, Rebecca mumbled in her sleep as her long slender arm reached out to encircle Claire's waist, pulling her closer. Claire settled into the embrace, keenly aware of the heat pressing against her back.

Her eyes stayed locked on the open window. Darkness gradually faded as dawn's golden light trickled in. The rays illuminated the edges of the mesh window before creeping into the tent. Once it touched her outstretched fingertips, she crawled out of their cocoon and pulled on her shorts, careful not to wake her sleeping wife.

The door flap purred as she unzipped it and stepped outside while casting furtive glances at Rebecca's sleeping form. Her dry, cracked lips moved as if she were talking to someone in a dream.

They were both weak, but Rebecca's health was declining much more rapidly than Claire's. Hunger and thirst consumed them. It had been five days since they last split a chocolate bar, their only remaining bit of food. They emptied the last of their carefully rationed water the night before, though Rebecca had insisted on Claire drinking most of that, as she had most days. Claire glared at the small waves lapping the edges of the shore, teasing her with their false offers of hydration.

Their rapid escape had left them with only the items in their backpacks. Claire couldn't remember how long they had been there but the dead cell phones, empty food wrappers, and a dry canteen had become useless. The romantic camping trip had morphed into a nightmare. They were only supposed to be gone for one night.

"Morning."

She turned around as Rebecca shuffled out of the tent. Her cheeks were rosy, flushed from fever.

"Morning, how do you feel?" Claire hurried over to steady her as she stumbled on the loose sand.

She regained her balance and shrugged Claire's hand off her arm. "Like shit. I see our friends are still hanging around." She gestured toward the mainland where a crowd of bloody, disease-riddled shells that used to be their neighbors and friends had gathered to stare out toward their island.

"I guess food is getting scarce there. Jesus. *Food*. We aren't even people anymore, just food…" Rebecca narrowed her eyes and tilted her head, "Think zombies can swim?"

"Maybe, but they would have done it by now, don't you think?" Claire, ever the optimist, pulled her gaze from the shoreline and looked up at her expectantly.

Rebecca kept her eyes locked on the creatures. "Hell if I know."

Claire helped Rebecca into a sitting position with her back against a palm tree before plopping herself down next to the sick woman. They sat, resting in the years of familiarity and comfort.

The wind continued to carry the horrific sounds from across the water. Sometimes, when the wind was low, they came on a whisper, floating through the air. When the wind was stronger, they pierced the space between them with a red-hot anger.

"I can't do this anymore." Rebecca sighed.

"Don't say that, baby. Someone will come, you'll see," She said as she put her arm around her, ignoring the heat waves coming off Rebecca's skin.

Rebecca shrugged her off, her voice raising. "They won't! Can't you see that? Shit, can't you see *that*?" She gestured toward the shore. "There is no one coming to save us! Jesus, Claire. Quit being so damn positive, just once." She paused to catch her breath.

Claire knew they were running out of time, but she had to keep hoping someone would save them. It's all they had left, besides each other. Hope. Surely the disease hadn't taken over *everything*.

Over the next few days they watched as more and more of the afflicted crowded the mainland's shore, facing their island. The screams dwindled to a trickle on the breeze, leaving only silence in their wake. Claire didn't think she'd ever miss those sounds until they were gone and they were left only with the gentle lapping of the waves on the shore, palm leaves rustling in the wind, and the ever-present flapping of the tent window covers.

Flap.

Ding.

Flap.

She slept with Rebecca's body next to her for two days before the putrid smells permeated the tent and Claire realized she was gone. The stench of her wife decaying. She couldn't even grieve, there were no more tears left in her thirst-ravaged body.

In and out of consciousness, she lay next to Rebecca's body, unable and unwilling to move either of them. Claire wrapped her frail fingers around the unmoving grey flesh that used to be Rebecca's hands. The hands that used to touch her, hold her tight, make her believe that they could do anything. The hands that caressed her face at night, until Claire would lean into her palm, lips touching the smooth skin while the scent of Rebecca's lavender lotion enveloped her.

The memory of lavender hung in the air as Claire closed her eyes one last time.

Flap.

Ding.

Flap.

Blood of the Rougarou

Charles died on a Wednesday.

The day had started fine. Great, even. After ten years, they still couldn't get enough of each other. Evangeline eventually pulled herself from Charles' arms, laughing as she jogged to the front door of their hut to relieve herself outside.

"I'll be back," she called over her shoulder.

Charles smiled, "Hurry, *sha.*"

The image of him laying on their pallet of old blankets, propped up on one arm with sex-tousled hair, was forever burned into her memory as the last time she would lay with him. By the time she returned, he had left the bed and started the coffee pot over a fire in the corner. If she had known it would be their last time, she would have pulled him back to bed and never let him leave.

But she didn't know, so they crawled into their clothes and took their coffee cups to the front porch. Charles plopped down in a sun-cracked plastic lawn chair and Evangeline sat on the bottom step, her feet dangling over the muddy green waters of the swamp below, her toes pushing ripples across the surface while silver minnows darted between her feet. As the sun rose and filtered through the trees above them, they spoke of their fishing plans.

It was on their way back home later that evening, with a sack full of alligator gar, wet jeans, and weary smiles on their faces, that it happened.

"You hear that?" Charles asked, stopping in his tracks and tilting his head.

"Hear what?" Evangeline continued walking; unaware he had stopped behind her.

When he didn't answer, she stopped and turned around, only then realizing she was a good ten feet in front of him. The setting sun threw copper and gold shadows between the roots of the tupelo trees as he examined them, peering into their depths. Soft, crunching noises came from within.

"It's prob'ly a possum, come on let's get. I'm hungry." Evangeline resumed walking. The long wooden gig in her hand bounced as she walked, the sharp points still glistening with bits of fish from their trip. She preferred gigging bullfrogs, but Lent called for fish, at least on Fridays.

With one last look into the growing darkness, Charles turned and followed her.

He had only taken a few steps when a loud crash erupted from the trees and a thunderous roar pierced the air. By the time Angeline could whip her head around to see what happened, a hairy creature had already sunk its teeth into Charles' shoulder. Taller than an average man, it stood on two powerful hind legs. Grey-brown fur covered its body and razor-sharp claws glinted in the early evening light. The animal jerked away from Charles' shoulder, bits of sinew and flesh stretching from Charles' skin to its sharp yellowed teeth.

A Rougarou.

They had been so distracted with Holy Week, that they forgot the number-one rule of the swamp: Don't go out at night during a full moon. And especially during Lent, when the Rougarou attacked anyone breaking the sacred practices.

Charles dropped the sack of fish he was carrying and tried to pull away, but the animal had already reached around to his exposed stomach and dug in with its claws.

Evangeline screamed, her grip tightening on the gig. She ran toward the Rougarou, desperate to save Charles. She was almost within reach when the animal eviscerated Charles' stomach with one jerk. Evangeline froze, her eyes locked on her lover's. Years passed between them, the good and the bad. Years she had thought would continue to stretch out ahead of them.

Charles screamed and the creature howled, voices joining in an unholy chorus. Intestines poured from the bloody hole in Charles' stomach and unraveled as they fell to the ground in front of him. Evangeline threw the gig as hard as she could at the Rougarou. The three sharp tines on the end of the wooden pole sunk into the soft flesh of the creature's cheek and it roared in pain before jerking the gig from its skin. Blood poured from the open holes. With one hand grasping its face, the Rougarou growled and ran off into the dense foliage.

Evangeline ran to Charles, dropping to her knees in the soft muck beside him. His open eyes were unfocused as blood drained from his wounds and his face paled. She scrambled to gather his intestines, but they slipped through her fingers like the muddy slime at the bottom of the swamp.

But it no longer mattered, he was gone.

Crying, Evangeline ripped a strip of cloth from the bottom of her shirt with shaking hands. She pressed it to his stomach and wrapped it around him, knotting it tight against his side to hold in the dirt-covered intestines she had managed to stuff back inside.

"Hang in there, Charles," she sobbed. "I'll get you back."

Looping her arms beneath his, Evangeline dragged his body the rest of the way to their raft at the edge of the swamp, leaving the bag of fish in a pool of blood behind them.

When she pulled the raft up to their dock, exhausted and covered in his blood, the night creatures had begun their swamp songs in the soft light of the full moon. Evangeline laid him gently on the floor in the center of their hut and collapsed next to him.

The next morning, she rummaged through her Great-Maw-Maw's chest, hoping for something to help Charles come back to her. Spellbooks and loose sheets with incantations surrounded her as she desperately continued her search. It *had* to be there, somewhere. There had to be a way to bring him back. But she had let herself forget too much since Maw-Maw's death, Evangeline was out of practice and at a loss for what to do.

She found it almost by accident when a single sheet fell from between the pages of one of the books and into her lap. Stained with time, her ancestor's handwriting described the exact spell Evangeline would need to perform. It didn't promise results, nothing ever did. But it was her only shot.

THURSDAY

The full moon hung low over the Bay Sirius Swamp, surrounded by stars brighter than any seen from town, unhindered by buildings or smog. Below moss-strung branches, rough bark dug into Evangeline's hands as she pressed herself flat against the trunk of a tree. She groaned as her feet slipped on the exposed moss-covered roots. Behind her, heavy footsteps thundered into a small clearing before coming to an abrupt stop. Evangeline held her breath and willed her heart to slow, sure the Rougarou could hear it straining against her chest, threatening to burst through.

Leaves rustled as the creature stepped closer to Evangeline's tree, sniffing and huffing. The swamp seemed to freeze around her; crickets and frogs ceased their songs and the murky water no longer lapped at the banks. Evangeline moved one foot to the side, easing it between roots so she could twist her body into position. With hands still gripping the tree, she risked a peek around the thick trunk.

The Rougarou was gone.

Evangeline strained to see through the trees on the other side of the clearing. She exhaled but it was a strange sound, amplified in the quiet swamp. Covered in sweat, she reached to wipe the moisture from the back of her neck when she felt it: hot breath on the back of her hand. Evangeline turned, and a scream caught in her throat. She was face-to-face with the massive, fur-covered Rougarou. Close enough to count the drops of saliva on the exposed fangs. Spit sprayed her face as the creature roared and lunged toward her. Screaming, Evangeline dove to the right as sharp claws scraped across her back. She scrambled to her feet and ran, sprinting alongside the bank of the swamp.

She was fast, but the Rougarou was faster. The great beast bellowed and the distance between them narrowed. Evangeline leapt across a fallen tree limb. Her feet landed in a scattering of leaves on the other side and she slid, narrowly missing a wide pile of dead branches. Skirting around the debris, she risked a glance over her shoulder. The Rougarou was still hot on her trail, leaping over the same fallen tree behind her before landing with a heavy thud. Recognition sparked in the creature's eyes. His cheek twitched and the three holes left by her gig there the day before danced behind crusted blood. A deep growl rumbled in the back of its throat.

Evangeline didn't dare move. His teeth gnashed as his hairy chest heaved and his long ears twitched backward. When the Rougarou stepped toward the edge of the pile of branches, they crunched beneath his feet. He pressed his heels into the ground and lowered his body. The fur rippled as the muscles tightened. He crouched low.

In one powerful burst, his hind legs pushed off the ground, arms outstretched with claws ready to rip through her flesh. It only took one step, one foot landing fully on top of the pile of branches, and he broke through them. The creature yelped in surprise as he plummeted to the bottom of the hole Evangeline had dug a few hours before. He roared and his hind legs scrambled for purchase against the muddy, slick walls of the homemade pit.

Evangeline stepped toward the edge and looked down. He was snarling and frantically trying to climb to his freedom. She bent down and, as her eyes remained locked on his, reached beneath a rock.

Earlier that morning, as she set her trap, she had hidden Charles' favorite machete. She gripped it as she stepped back from the pit's opening, breaking eye contact while she allowed the Rougarou to continue his efforts. Finally, pointed ears emerged. Then wide bloodshot eyes, a long snout, and yellowed fangs. She tightened her grip on the machete. When the chin and then the thick neck cleared the opening, Evangeline swung the sharp blade sideways, slicing off the head of the Rougarou. It flew through the air, trailing bits of flesh and blood behind it as it landed on the ground near her, still growling and gnashing its teeth.

In the pit, the body of the creature fell once again to the damp earth at the bottom of the hole. The long claws retracted back into its hands and shrunk to the size of fingernails. Its skin shuddered as it absorbed the fur, leaving nothing but smooth flesh behind.

Evangeline spit into the hole and muttered, "Good riddance, *chen sal*," before tossing the now-silent head into a sack and turning toward the water's edge.

She couldn't believe the trap worked. Not that she ever doubted Charles, his skills as a hunter were known throughout Butte La Rose Parish. She did, however, doubt her ability to do it without him. If only he were there to see her.

But soon.

Muscles aching and shrouded in the pale glow of the waning gibbous moon, Evangeline began the long trek back to her hut. A dense fog crawled from the swamp waters and licked at her feet as the crickets and bullfrogs cried out to her along the way.

FRIDAY

Early in the morning, just past night's darkest hour when the sky turned from ink to gray, Evangeline finally stepped onto the creaking boards of the dock that led to her front door.

Charles was still there on the floor, smelling worse than the day before and gathering flies. His *ti bon-ange* was still intact, but she knew she had to work fast before his soul left for good.

As she washed and prepared him for the ritual, her hands passed over his tanned chest. Perhaps if he hadn't insisted on going shirtless, the Rougarou wouldn't have done as much damage. But then again, getting Charles to wear a shirt proved near impossible even on a good day.

His excuse was always, "*Cher*, who do I have to impress out here? The crawdads? The gators?"

Leaving the wrapping around his stomach, Evangeline dabbed at the crusted blood on his skin with a wet rag. Her sorrow deepened when he didn't flinch as she cleaned the bite wound on his shoulder. He was more dead than she cared for, but it still wasn't an impossible task. She tossed the rag into a bucket in the corner of the hut, grabbed her scissors, and came back to Charles' side. She ran her fingers through his thick hair, previously black but with the beginnings of a nice "salt-and-pepper" look that he would have grown into handsomely. At the very back of his neck, where he wouldn't miss it, Evangeline snipped a bundle of hair no bigger than her thumb. She placed it on a nearby table then turned back to his body with a heavy sigh.

He looked so peaceful, as if he were simply taking a nap. She tugged on the blood-soaked cloth around his body. He could spare a tiny piece of the cotton. If he knew what she was doing, she was sure he'd be willing to spare the entire thing, allowing himself to spill onto the floor of their hut. But then again, he always did leave messes for her to clean up. No matter, she loved him and needed him back. With her scissors and a steady hand, Evangeline cut a piece of bloody cloth from the wrapping, tore it into three long pieces, then braided them together.

Hanging over the fire in the corner was her Great-Maw-Maw's cast-iron pot. In it sat a small beeswax-filled tin with a few inches of water between the tin and the sides of the pot. She tied a small rock to the end of the braided cloth then dropped it into the wax where it bubbled and swayed in the hot liquid. When it was sufficiently coated, she pulled it from the pot with a pair of tongs, dipped it into a tub of cool swamp water sitting on the floor, and placed it on the table.

Charles was ready. The wick was ready. Crawfish lungs, sage, crow feathers, nutria rat bones, and chicken feet covered her table. She only needed the blood of the creature who had killed him. The Rougarou's head sat in a bin on the edge of her table, silent and musky. The copper odor of blood permeated the small hut. Evangeline dipped into the bottom of the bin with a small cup and filled it with the Rougarou's blood. Holding her breath, she poured it into the bubbling beeswax along with the rest of the ingredients from the table and stirred it all with a wooden spoon until everything glistened in the hot wax.

Pinching the very tip of the wick, Evangeline lowered the wax-coated braid into the pot. When the weight at the other end broke the surface, the potion hissed and gurgled. She held her breath and dipped all but the top two inches of the wick into the wax, then moved it to a jug of cooled water on the dirt floor beside her. She repeated this motion exactly thirteen more times before hanging the candle from a nail on the front porch to harden. Thin white slivers of crawfish lungs, broken feathers, and bones stuck out from the sides of the candle.

While the wax set, Evangeline drew a circle in Rougarou blood around Charles' body. She then covered the windows with old sheets, blocking out all outside light. Once the candle was ready, she carried it back inside and lit the top of the wick with a match. The flame sputtered and danced before finding its strength and chasing away the pitch-black darkness inside the hut.

Evangeline took a deep breath and grabbed the ancient paper with her Great Maw-Maw's writing on it. The Creole script seemed to pulsate in her hand. With trembling breath, she read the first few lines from the paper then paused to drip candle wax onto Charles' forehead. Murmuring the words again, she spilled more wax onto his chest, over his heart. Charles seemed to inhale, and she couldn't tell if his skin shuddered around the wax, or if the dancing candlelight was playing tricks on her.

She continued reading and dripping wax down his body.

It wasn't until she slipped the cloth wrapping down, revealing his open wound, that she knew it was no longer just the candlelight. As the hot wax hit his raw flesh, he groaned. Evangeline hurried through the rest of the ritual, snuffed the candle out, and yanked the coverings from the windows.

She leaned against the edge of the table, closed her eyes, and prayed.

With a gasp, Charles' eyes flew open and he scrambled to his feet, panting. Evangeline cried out and took a step toward him before freezing. He had changed. She thought it might happen, but had hoped the Voodoo was strong enough to counter the Rougarou's bite. But there he was, morphing into the very creature that had attacked him. She stumbled back against the side of the hut as his head swung toward her and he snarled. His once-soft and tender brown eyes were wide and bloodshot. His nails elongated and sharpened into claws and his skin shuddered as hair protruded from its surface.

Evangeline reached behind her, keeping her eyes on the fast-approaching Charles-creature. Her fingers landed on the pot. She gripped the handle and swung the heavy pot in a wide arc, meeting his head with a crack. He stumbled before falling to the floor in a heap.

Tears streaming down her face, Evangeline set to work.

***

The pot, cleaned of wax and filled with Gumbo Z'Herbes, simmered over the fire in the corner of the hut. Charles lay propped up on their pallet of blankets, eyes focused on nothing and a dumb smile on his face.

"You're going to love this, it might be my best one yet," She said as she brought a spoonful to his mouth. "Here, taste."

Charles eased his hands toward the spoon with great effort, but stopped just short and stared at her. Blood-soaked bandages covered both of his hands. His spoon-holding and self-feeding days were long gone.

"No, of course you can't. Here." Evangeline placed the spoon in his mouth and tilted.

Gumbo spilled from the edges of his mouth, mixed with blood and saliva. She had hit him harder than she meant to and, judging from the bits of brain showing through the gash on the back of his head, he wouldn't quite be the same Charles she was used to. It was like feeding a baby, she imagined. Not that they ever had a baby.

Not yet.

She cleaned him up and lay next to him, watching her hand on his chest rising and falling with each breath. At least he was alive.

Mostly.

In the corner of their hut lay a pile of pointed yellow teeth and sharp claws with the tips of Charles' fingers still attached. Brain-damaged or not, she couldn't fight him off every time there was a full moon. Rougarous were dangerous creatures.

Even the Jellyfish

Jellyfish lay dead on the sand, just beyond the surf's reach. Remember how the grit covered their once-purple bodies, leaving them nothing more than dirty, deflated bubbles? It's possible you didn't see them; your eyes were full of light back then and shining on me. Or maybe you don't remember those dirty blobs on the sand at all. But they were there, waiting for someone to step on them and feel their not-long-dead-but-still-painful sting.

We walked into the breaking waves until water crept up to our waists and we squealed with the cold shock of it, even though it brought a welcome relief from the raging sun above. You laughed that magnificent laugh of yours and dove beneath a wave. For a minute I couldn't see you, but your black hair broke the surface after the wave finished rushing over you, and around me. You rubbed the water from your eyes before opening them, eager to see if I had gone under with you, but I didn't. I should have.

Do you remember floating on our backs and holding hands while we watched the pelicans fly beneath the clouds? We were past the second sandbar so the waves no longer crashed against us but undulated beneath. You told me that bull sharks had no problem swimming in shallow water and could be below us at that very moment. I told you about a jellyfish next to us, and we let go of each other's hands as we swam away. Maybe the bull shark moved with us, you said before pulling me closer and kissing me there in the low swells and salty air. A boat horn echoed in the distance and a mullet splashed nearby, but we only caught a glimpse of its silver tail as it slipped beneath the surface.

It was a perfect day, preceded and followed by many other perfect days. Seeing you in this chair, in this place, has me reminiscing. A garishly bright sign above the nurse's station announces a "Tiki Party" so maybe that's what brought me back to the beach, with you. Anywhere but this quiet room where life seems to stall. Sunlight filters in through heavy drapes and two old men slowly play checkers behind us. The "clack-clack" of the pieces is almost keeping beat with the soft music coming from the speakers in the ceiling.

I lean close to you and whisper, "I love you."

You stare at me through time-clouded eyes, confused. Clutching the blanket in your lap, you look around for the nurse.

I miss you.

I miss the sand, the waves, and the mullet. I miss the boat even though it interrupted our embrace. I miss the clouds and the pelicans. And if it meant I could go back to that day with you one more time, I even miss the jellyfish.

Step Right Up

Yellow-haired girls with pink bows laugh and clutch lollipops the size of their heads.

Young lovers shuffle down the midway hand in hand.

Boys with mischievous glints in their eyes run as the sunlight sparkles off their freshly shined shoes.

All here for the show. My show. I like to think of it as mine. It's as much a part of me as that bow is a part of the little girl standing in line for her ticket. The girl's mother reins her in with a tight grip as the child pulls forward, eager to see around my booth.

Even after everything that has happened, I know I belong here. I search each of my customers for some connection, something tying me to people so foreign, yet who could easily be me. They could have been born under the Big Top, backstage where the roar of the crowd on the other side of the curtain drowned out their first cry. They could have taken their first breath of air saturated with peanut dust, wayward bits of hay, and the scent of popping corn. They could have reached up to yank their mother's curly beard while suckling at her breast, giggling as she pretended the tiny tug actually hurt.

But I know they didn't. They were born in hospitals, breathing stale air and shivering in frigid rooms. Their mothers didn't have beards and their fathers wouldn't know how to glide through the air. Sounds incredibly dull if you ask me. But people can't help what they're born into.

My papa says they're dull people, trying to brighten up their dull lives with a glimpse into ours. But I find them fascinating: Old, young, dark, pale, ecstatic, morose. All of them come through with stories and lives so different from my own, like the people in the pile of books in my tent. Exotic and intriguing.

As the line shuffles past, a group of boys with shiny shoes step up, puffing out their chests in the way that only young-boys-almost-men can. My brother used to strut around like that.

Unlike the crowds before them, these boys look me squarely in the eye. But I don't want to play their game. I avert my gaze, pull their crisp bills through the gap, and slide four tickets under the glass. They aren't the first to poke fun at me for living here, or for being who I am. I get enough of that from my family.

Mama can't hide her pity as she strokes my face, tsking as if being normal was some fault of my own, before leaning down to kiss me on my bare cheek. Her love isn't dependent on her daughter becoming the next Bearded Lady. It would have been okay for me to have a smooth chin uncovered by curly brown hair if I only had other talents. But as I grew older, my parents' hope for some sign that I was destined for greatness dwindled to nothing. The daughter of The Bearded Lady and Zanos the Flyer? Why *wouldn't* they expect great things? My brother Tormund certainly turned out all right. He can't fly like Papa, but at least he has a little talent. They say he can chuck knives better than the Gibsons over at Ringling Brothers. I say until he perfects the Wheel of Death, he can't hold a candle to the Gibsons, but Mama always hushes me right about then.

I can't throw knives, even after years of denting Tormund's practice set. He was mad about that for a while until Papa finally bought him new ones.

My attempts at flying were even worse, mama made papa stop pushing me after two broken ankles and a fractured collarbone. I'm not pretty enough to ride the elephants and I'm too shy to be a clown, so I just sit in the ticket booth and watch the norms file past.

It's not a terrible life, not even a boring one. I like to watch the girls skipping in their frilly dresses, excited to see the shows without a care in the world. I don't own a dress, not anymore. Hand-me-down jeans and overalls are all I need. I stare at the parents with toddlers in tow, eager to show them the wonders within. Different from my own mama and papa, but an intense love all the same.

What I don't like are the packs of boys looking for trouble. Like the ones still standing in front of my window.

"I bet she's a freak," mutters a boy with gel-saturated black hair and a cold grin.

The shortest, a redhead with a smattering of freckles across his nose, stares at me through the window and answers with disdain, "Don't look like much of a freak."

A third boy on the other side of my door wriggles the doorknob. "I bet she's got three titties. Come on, give us a look!"

As if that's original. I hear that at least twice in every town.

I sigh and look around them hoping for another customer, but the field is empty. The shows have started, and the latecomers have all skittered away to their seats. It's just the boys and me alone at this end of the fairway.

In the distance, I hear Master Liman's bullhorn-amplified voice announce the start of "The Most Magnificent Show on Earth." The double-paned glass in my booth rattles, signaling the entrance of Topsy, Mary, and Rosie, the Asian elephants.

But the boys remain. Three in front of my window and one on the side, hand still jiggling the door. I shuffle the dollar bills and ignore their taunts as music floats around us, carried on the breeze across a grass ocean from the Big Top's show. Flowers dance in the wind, pushing and pulling to the beat of the drums that have now entered the chorus. A symphony to which I will never dance, or ride, or fly.

But I have no regrets, for I do have a skill that no one will *ever* know about. Two years ago when I was twelve, I broke my left ankle after another unsuccessful attempt at flying. My arms were sore from hobbling around on crutches, so I had taken to sitting in the field behind the big tent, far away from my papa's disappointed looks. With nothing to do but rest and read my books, it was my favorite place in the world.

Until one hazy day in April, when the clouds were pregnant with rain and threatening to birth any moment. I was pulling myself up with the crutches and gathering my things to go back inside when Louis, Master Liman's sixteen-year-old son, noticed me from across the field. He jogged over and smiled, perfect white teeth behind perfect lips. Lord, he sure was handsome back then.

"Hey, watcha doin' way over here?" he asked, standing closer to me than any boy who wasn't my brother had before.

I was suddenly very aware of my heartbeat.

"Nothing," I muttered, struggling to appear cool despite the red-hot warmth spreading across my face.

Louis reached out his hand and grabbed my waist, drawing me closer to him. My crutches clattered to the ground, and I leaned forward to keep from following them. Our hips touched and the heat from his body seeped into mine like a virus, pushing my blood faster through my veins.

He lifted my chin with his other hand and pressed his lips against mine. I held my lips together, but his teeth forced their way through, piercing and hard. His arm was around my back, holding me captive. I tried to scream but opening my mouth seemed to signal to him I wanted the kiss, wanted him inside my body.

When he finally pulled away, I thought he would leave me alone and go back to his friends. I could see them watching us, peeking out from around the elephant stalls and laughing. It was a joke. No one would want to spend time with me except as part of a cruel prank. But he didn't leave me alone.

He shoved me down into the tall grass and fell on top of me, forcing the breath from my lungs. He covered my mouth with one hand as I stared at him, eyes wide and pleading. With the other, he pulled my dress up around my waist, ripping it. On quiet nights I can still hear the fabric tearing.

I couldn't scream, not that anyone would hear me if I did. Except his friends who were probably still laughing as they watched us. When Louis entered me, a rock shifted beneath my back, turning its sharp side to my flesh and scraping my tender skin through the shards of my dress. I kept my eyes closed and thought of that rock and the hole it would make in the fabric, in my skin. Anything that would take me away from what was happening on top of me.

That's when the rains came, soaking both of us. But that didn't deter him. He finished and stood, pulling up his trousers and smiling at me as he buckled his belt. Even after he was long gone, I remained in the mud and grass with that rock stabbing at my back and my crutches next to me. I knew what had just happened, but I couldn't believe it. I grew up with Louis; we were practically cousins. But the blood and semen on my thigh, the ache inside, and the horror of it all said it had definitely happened.

I pulled myself together and hobbled back to our tent, terrified and confused. It wasn't until later that the festering anger seeped in and settled in my stomach like a squatter in a broken, decrepit house.

"Where have you been?!" My papa had seethed, screaming through his teeth. That was a particular skill of his, yelling at you without anyone hearing. "Peasey needs help in the kitchen, and we've been looking everywhere for you! Now go get changed and head over there." He pushed me toward the curtain that separated my sleeping mat from the rest of the tent.

"But papa . . ." I started. Couldn't he see the tears and the ripped dress and the shock of it all on my face?

"No buts, young lady. Get yourself cleaned up. Just look at you! No telling what you've been doing in them fields all day, coming back soaked and all muddy. You just wait till I tell your mama about this."

And he was gone, his threats trailing after him as he disappeared into the gloomy afternoon.

Later that night, once the chores were done and everyone was settling in, I told Mama what happened out there in that field. She tucked my blanket around my chin and promised she would take care of me, her tears falling onto my face and mingling with my own. I drifted off to sleep amongst hushed whispers between her and Papa, waking only when he touched my arm.

"I'm so sorry. I'm so sorry, I didn't know," he whispered, though his voice cracked and shattered like a broken mirror. "I'm gonna make this right, I swear to you."

And he tried, but Louis denied everything, and Master Liman believed his only son, his heir. Louis was training to be the next Ringmaster when Liman retired. The future–our future–was riding on Louis' shoulders. Who was I compared to that, but a girl with no talents that no one believed?

Well, almost no talents.

About a week later, I bumped into Louis at the edge of Clown Alley. He grinned and patted me on the shoulder like we were two old pals. When he passed me, he reached out and slapped my bottom, cupping his hand before strutting off like he already owned the place. Like he owned *me*.

But I was no longer scared. A low heat rumbled across my body, and I shook all over. As he sauntered off, all the rage and hurt from the past week rolled like a fever in my chest. I could still feel him inside me, his weight pushing on me, unable to breathe, much less scream. I hated him. I hated what he thought he could get away with.

If only he had asked for a blowjob just then, I would have bitten his penis clean off and smiled while I spit it out onto the ground. He would have tried to stop me, but I would have bitten down harder and pulled my head back, his flesh ripping away from his body, his blood spurting down my face and neck, pooling in the small indentions above my collar bones and running down my chest.

Louis stopped and grabbed his crotch with both hands before dropping to the ground with a groan. His face was white as Ringo's just before a show, but instead of a beaming clown grin painted on, his mouth gaped open. It looked like he was trying to scream, but he only got out a whimper. I took a step toward him, and his eyes darted toward mine and widened, terrified. Blood seeped out from the inside of his pants, creeping along the edges of his hands still clutched there. Knowing I did it, but not understanding how, I was almost ashamed at how much joy I was taking in his suffering.

Almost.

I turned from the spectacle to look around; it was just us in the alley. With a satisfied grin I walked away, leaving him in the dirt with a growing puddle of urine and blood seeping out of his breeches.

They found him in time to save his life. If they had been but a few minutes later, everyone was sure he would have bled to death. No one could figure out what happened, and Louis wouldn't say. He'd just sit in his trailer in the dark, mourning the loss of his manhood that they weren't able to reattach. Our doctor was also our vet, and not as skilled with the sewing-back-on of private parts as perhaps some big city doctors were.

So now, two years after that day in Clown Alley, I keep my secret as Louis has always kept his. If Master Liman found out, I would be stuck inside a tent all day, forced to perform. Or he would kick my parents and me out. Knowing Liman and how much he liked his money; I'd bet on him keeping us.

But I'd much rather be in my ticket booth where, although small, the windows are large and allow me to look for miles around. I get to watch people, try to figure out their stories and, while the shows are going on, read my books by the light of a small lamp. I get to do what I want and see the world whoosh by as our train chugs from town to town.

Most days.

Today, these boys are interfering with my reading time. They should be in the big tent with the rest of the customers. They egg each other on to say the crudest, most vile things they can think of, all the while still trying to get into my booth.

With a crack, the knob finally stops moving and the door swings inward. A tan boy with wavy brown hair grins at me, his hand still on the door-knob.

I ease off the stool and take a step back, not breaking his stare. That same white-hot fury builds in my chest, and I want to see just how far I can take this talent of mine. I imagine grabbing his arm, the one that is still resting on the door handle. Pushing down on it until I can hear the bones crack in the back of my mind. His smile turns to confusion as he screams and looks down. His hand is no longer resting on the door handle, and both of the bones below his elbow are sticking out of his arm, their jagged white edges shining in stark contrast with his tan skin.

Seeing their friend enter my booth, the other boys had whooped and hollered, excited for a little action. Hearing his screams, they're now confused. But I'm not finished just yet.

As the boy runs off holding his arm, two of his friends follow him. One of them, the one who claimed I had "three titties," stays behind, staring at me. In that cocked head and raised eyebrow, he seems to look into my soul and see what I am capable of. But, like most young boys who see a fence and need to climb it, he has to see for himself.

I sigh and stare back at him. Fine. If he wants to see a show, I'll give him a show. He did buy a ticket, after all.

I glare at him through the dusty glass and picture a fat cigar, the kind Master Liman likes to hang from his mouth, hardly ever smoking it. But now the cigar is lit, burning and sizzling as it presses into the boy's chest, perfectly centered between his hairless nipples. He screams and spins around, grabbing at his shirt. I press harder as he runs to catch up to his friends, searing the skin good, making sure there will be a scar. Now *he'll* be the one with three nipples.

They almost trip over a young couple walking toward my booth, arms intertwined and late for the show.

"Everything all right there?" the man asks, gesturing toward the boys.

"Oh yeah, they'll be fine."

He pushes his ten dollars beneath the glass and I smile at him, passing the tickets through.

"Enjoy the show."

How to Pose the Dead

Jessica Barlowe didn't set out that morning with the intention of killing six people, but sometimes there's just so much bullshit a woman can take before she starts itchin' to give a little of it back.

She was standing by her car at The Smiling Oaks, her least favorite photography location, waiting for her client to show up. If their earlier communications were any indicator, she knew this particular client would be a pain in her ass. Jessica pulled her phone out, glared at the time, and shoved it back in her pocket. The summer sun beat down on her, and she could already feel the first drops of sweat building on the back of her neck. She knew the minute she climbed back into her Corolla and turned on the air conditioner, the client would pull up and she'd have to get out, re-adjust the camera around her neck and the other one hanging from her shoulder, and wait ten minutes for both lenses to defog. Fucking Texas summers. If the heat and humidity didn't kill you, the mosquitos would. It was her least favorite time to shoot, but the most profitable. That is, when people showed up for their photo sessions, anyway.

The Smiling Oaks was started by Pam Jeffries as a way for local photographers to have more options for their backdrops. The main attractions were the Oak trees (hence the name). Two-hundred-year-old Oaks dominated the landscape, dripping with Spanish Moss that longed for a breeze in the stifling summer heat.

Jessica shifted her weight to her other leg, wiped the sweat off her forehead, and stared down the long caliche driveway. She calculated the time she would need later to get ready for her date. It was her first real date since the divorce. She had a few drinks with her cousin's friend the week before, but the guy was a bore, so she didn't count it. Talked incessantly about stupid shit. She had excused herself to use the restroom and snuck out a back door. But this one, this was a real date. She had shaved her legs for this one.

Jason was a musician, she met him at an open mic night down at Wayside Pub in Lake Jackson. He was from New Orleans, had evacuated to Texas from Hurricane Katrina, and never looked back. He played piano in that sultry, New Orleans blues style that stirred things in her she hadn't felt since...well she couldn't remember. Adrian, her ex-husband, had definitely lacked in the passion department. His idea of a hot date was eating take-out in front of the TV and falling asleep to *Law and Order* reruns. Good riddance to him, that sorry excuse for a man. But if he thought he was sticking her with the mortgage, he had another thing coming. Like she wanted to keep living three houses down from his mother. Cut the fucking umbilical cord already, Jesus Christ. For all she cared, he could go ahead and suck on the tit 'til he was seventy, it was no longer her problem.

She needed this date. She *deserved* this date. Not that she was looking for anything serious, but damn if she didn't have some itches that needed scratching.

Jessica glanced again at her phone. The client was now thirty minutes late, and Jessica had only booked one hour. The holy roller that ran The Smiling Oaks charged thirty bucks an hour for a bunch of old trees, dumbass signs, and various shit made out of whatever was on sale at Hobby Mart.

She hated shooting there. Not that anyone bothered her. Pam Jeffries tended to stay indoors, especially in the summer. Their house was about a stone's throw from the gated entrance to the "Field of Bullshit." That's what Jessica called it, anyway. Cutesy, country-ass setups that were extremely popular with the local small-town moms.

It was all just a bit too much. Jessica believed in the "less is more" mentality. Let the focus be on the subjects, that's what they were there for anyway. Not the bullshit cluttered backgrounds. But the client got what the client wanted, and Jessica sucked it up if she wanted to keep paying her bills.

Not that The Smiling Oaks was the only headache in her photography business. Even when she was at the beach, downtown, in a field, or at the old Plantation House, the moms irritated her. Always the moms, hardly ever anyone else. If Jessica saw one more baby with a blinged-out bow bigger than their head, she was going to scream. Or a request for selective coloring on a final print. Sure, she could make everything black and white except for that bouquet of roses, she loved to make pictures look like they were taken in 1984 by the department store photographers. And that sheet of poses printed off the internet? Sure, she simply adored being told how to do her job. Of course, that pose looked natural, people often leaned against their partner as they both made a heart with their hands over a pregnant belly.

Jessica took one last look down the driveway and wiped her neck. She was sweating like a whore in church.

"Fuck this, I'm out."

She pulled the cameras off, set them on her backseat, and started her car. Just as she was backing up, a red Ford tumbled down the road. The white rocks crunched beneath the wheels and a fine plume of dust shot out from behind the car. It stopped just behind Jessica, blocking her in.

She took a deep breath, pulled back into her parking spot, and retrieved her cameras from the back seat.

The doors on the Ford swung open and a crowd of people spilled out of it like it was Octomom's vagina. They were all full of smiles and laughs, noticeably lacking in time awareness or apologies.

Jessica forced a smile. "You made it! I was just about to head on out."

"Oh, are we late? Goodness, you know me — Miss Scatterbrain!" Her client, Karen Miller, waved her hand in the air above her head.

"Ready to get started? We don't have that much time left in our slot."

"Oh, those things are just suggestions anyway, we'll be fine," Karen answered before looking around. "I don't even see anyone outside, how are they gonna know if we take a little longer? No one cares."

Well, *she* cared. Jason was meeting her at Mikel's Pub at 8:00.

Before Jessica could respond, Karen continued, "Is there somewhere to change clothes? We brought a few different outfits; I hope you brought lots of film!" Karen had jokes. Jessica didn't use film and hadn't since about 2004. She had digital cameras. Karen knew that.

"I'm sorry, you said you only wanted one outfit, that's why we only booked one hour for your family portraits."

"It won't take long, we'll be real quick, I promise."

"Let's just start with what y'all have on right now."

Next to Karen, a tall balding man lit a cigarette and played on his phone. Jessica presumed him to be Karen's husband, due to the utter lack of give-a-fuck in his eyes. Only someone like that could be married to someone like her.

"Douglas, can you at least tuck in your shirt? Lord, I swear you'd think he was born in a barn," Karen said.

He didn't look up from his phone as he held the cigarette between his lips and shoved the yellow and white plaid shirt into his jeans with his free hand. Behind him, two women were adjusting each other's clothing and hair. The daughter and the daughter-in-law, Jessica assumed. The tall one, a bleach-blond with an inch of dark brown roots, had the same unfortunate dopey look as her father. She was squeezed into a too-small yellow shirt with holes cut out of the top of the shoulders. A replica of the one her mother, Karen, wore. The shorter woman had tightly cropped black hair and wore a fitted suit jacket over a yellow tank top with dark jeans, not exactly matching the country bling of the rest of the family.

Those people Jessica expected. They were the ones she was getting paid to photograph. The unexpected ones, the people she had *not* agreed to photograph, had gone to the fence line to look at a Quarter horse grazing by the fence. A teenage boy watched as a woman who looked to be in her mid-forties reached over the fence to try to pet the horse. It snorted at her in disdain before trotting off. Jessica wished she could be more like that horse.

Sometimes clients brought other people to the photo shoots to help out or just for moral support, but the boy also wore a yellow and white plaid shirt, and the woman was in a yellow sun dress. Fan-fucking-tastic.

Jessica turned to Karen, raising an eyebrow.

"Oh yeah, I figured we could just take a couple with my cousin and her kid, just a few quick snaps since we're here. You don't mind, right?" She turned toward the woman and boy. "Bethany! Stevie! Y'all come on over here and meet Jessica."

Even though Karen had only paid for a session with her immediate family. But sure, she'd love to have more outfits and people to photograph in half the time. She was definitely going to ask that bitch for more money, and Karen would pay it, or she wouldn't see any pictures.

Jesus H. Christ, she needed another job. But she had yet to find something she was qualified for that would require zero interaction with other humans.

Jessica took a deep breath, put on her best "pretend to give a fuck so she could just get out of there and get to her date" face, and walked toward the entrance to the garden.

She called over her shoulder, "Let's go ahead and start here."

Karen followed. "We're ready and rarin' to go!"

Jessica rolled her eyes.

At the entrance to the garden, a stone pathway led up to a white gazebo. Delicate lace-work designs were etched into the wooden support beams and a string of fairy lights draped across the ceiling. Colorful pots overflowing with pink Begonias and purple Petunias framed the steps.

Jessica turned to Karen. "Okay, why don't we start with just you and your husband?"

"I hope you got a backup there, wouldn't want this face to break your camera!" Douglas chortled.

Jessica patted the second camera hanging from her arm. "That's what this one is for." Her smile didn't climb up to her eyes, she had already heard that same joke four times that week.

"Be sure you get my good side!" Karen smiled.

"I'll get all your good sides," Jessica answered with her standard response and another forced smile.

The clock was ticking, Jason was waiting, and she didn't have time or energy for bullshit.

After twenty minutes of Karen and her daughter, Debbie, directing the photoshoot, assuming they knew more than Jessica about lighting, over-dramatizing the few mosquitos that were present, and repeatedly telling Stevie to put down his phone, Jessica was pretty much done.

"Look we only have a few minutes, want to do some of the whole family over on that stage real quick?"

"You can hold your horses. Hun, I'm paying a lot of money for this, and I won't have you rushing me."

"Yes ma'am, but you were a little late-"

"I already done told you that don't matter. Now come on I'm wilting over here. I'm payin' for an hour and I'm gettin' an hour."

Jessica looked to Debbie and Douglas for help. They averted their eyes, pretending to look at their phones.

Jessica gritted her teeth and smiled at Karen, "Let's go to the stage over there." She knew she should have asked for the payment upfront instead of at the end of the session.

The relentless sun beat down on the group as they continued down the pathway to a wooden platform set at the back of the garden. It wasn't the dumbest prop Jessica had ever come across, but it was right down there with the bottom five. Center stage were three large door frames with gilded edges and elaborate designs. Each frame balanced on a wooden base. Jessica never understood what it was supposed to be or why anyone would want to photograph it.

"Oh my god, I can*not* believe this!" Debbie screamed as she reached the top step and looked down at her shirt. She turned to Jessica, "I told you I didn't want to lean on that dirty gazebo and just look what happened!"

The sleeve of her shirt had a single thread sticking out. One. Single. Thread. When her wife moved to pull the thread out, Debbie slapped her hand away.

"No, you'll make a hole!"

Karen rushed to her daughter's side to console her, and both murmured about having a photographer who asked them to lean on things, ruining their best church clothes.

"Oh, for fuck's sake," Jessica turned to Douglas. "Do you have a pocketknife?"

He nodded, pulled the knife from his pocket, and handed it to Jessica.

She unfolded the knife and walked over to where Karen and Debbie were standing. Their eyes widened at the sight of the sharp blade, but before they could back away, Jessica snipped off the offending thread with a flick of her wrist.

"I think you'll live."

Karen gasped and whispered to her daughter loud enough for everyone to hear, "Well, *that* was uncalled for."

Jessica shoved the knife in her pocket, took a deep breath, and called the rest of the family up on the stage. By the time they finished, everyone was dabbing sweat from their foreheads and ballooning out their shirts to fan themselves.

"Ok so I think we're good-"

"What about that tree over there, can we take just one more there?" Karen asked. Debbie nodded in agreement.

Jessica sighed, "Sure, just one more."

"Hot enough for ya?" joked Douglas. As if he hadn't been saying that every five minutes for the past hour.

Past the stage was one of the biggest oak trees on the property. A thick branch swayed toward the ground. Moms loved getting shots of their toddlers sitting on it without a worry at all that the kid would fall. It was Jessica's least favorite spot. The branches filtered the sunlight, leaving dappled hot spots on her client's faces. She preferred that natural look, but her clients hated it, so Jessica was forced to use an assortment of scrims and reflectors to even out the patchy light. She had left them in the car that day.

"For this spot, I'll need a few things from my car. Give me a minute."

"Oh no you don't, I know you're just trying to get out of here."

"Damn it, Karen. Let the woman do her job." Douglas piped up, surprising everyone.

Karen stared at her husband. Her eyes narrowed. "*Douglas*. Why don't you make yourself useful and retrieve her items for her?"

"It's really okay-"

"Hun, let him do *something*, at least." Karen leaned forward and whispered, "I swear sometimes he's about as useful as tits on a boar hog."

"I'm gonna go burn one, y'all figure it out." Douglas walked back through the garden toward the cars.

If looks could kill, Douglas would have dropped right then and there from the expression on his wife's face.

Karen huffed before turning back to the others, "Stevie, why don't you go get Jessica's stuff from her car while we take a few pictures here with just me and the girls, then."

Jessica knew she was cornered. She really wasn't planning on cutting out of there. Probably. Not before she got her money, anyway. She pulled her keys from her pocket and tossed them to the boy. "It's a black bag in the trunk. Thanks."

"No problem," he mumbled as he caught the keys and turned to go.

Before he was out of hearing distance, Karen turned to her daughter. "That boy couldn't hit the floor if he fell out of bed. We'll see what he actually comes back with."

Her cousin frowned, "Now Karen, that's not nice-"

"Oh my god, I'm just *kidding*! Why is everyone so serious today?" Karen laughed.

A shrill ringtone interrupted her. Her daughter-in-law glanced down at the caller id and turned to her wife. "Sorry babe, it's work."

"Are you serious right now? Can't you just go one minute without being on that damn phone?"

"I have to take it."

"No, you don't."

"I'm taking it," she replied as she walked away, the phone already up to her ear.

Debbie turned to her mom. "Can you believe this? You know what, *no*. She can't just keep doing this. I'll be right back," before following the other woman toward the fence line.

"They'll be fine, come take our picture. Hurry we're getting eaten alive out here," Karen swatted a mosquito on her arm, then wiped the bloody mess on the branch next to her.

Jessica started to respond, remembered the negative balance in her bank account, and bit her tongue.

The lowest branch of the giant oak tree curved down from the rest and sat on the grass, so the women leaned against the curve, put their arms around each other, and smiled at Jessica.

"Can you only take from here up? I'm still trying to lose a few pounds." Bethany gestured to an imaginary line slightly above her waist. "And can you take off about twenty pounds in Photoshop? That's not hard, right? And can you whiten my teeth?"

"Ooh, me too!" Karen said.

Bank account, thought Jessica. *Bank account*. "Sure."

Behind the women, a broken branch hung awkwardly, throwing a backdrop of dead brown leaves behind them.

"Hold on a sec, let me move this." Jessica walked behind the women, and they watched as she tugged on the dead branch, releasing it from its hold, before flinging it to the ground a few feet away.

The women fluffed their hair and turned back around. "Can you hurry? I'm melting over here," whined Karen.

"Yeah, can we pick this up a tad? We don't have all day," Bethany said.

Jessica stayed silent and remained planted behind them, staring at the sweat stains pooling at their backs and beneath their arms. Mosquitos swirled around her ankles, biting through her socks even though she had put on the highest-strength bug spray she could find. Jessica pulled the knife from her pocket and unfolded it. She ran her thumb along the sharp tip, leaving tiny dots of blood along her skin. Echoes of ten years of rude, entitled clients swarmed her thoughts.

The women continued talking about her as if she weren't standing right there behind them.

Bethany whispered loud enough for Jessica to hear, "I mean, really. How hard can it be anyway? Just point the camera and push a button. Next time let's have Margie's daughter take them with her phone. She's going to school for art, you know-"

She gurgled and gasped, clutching her neck. Karen turned to face her cousin, and her eyes widened. Bethany still leaned against the tree branch but had both hands wrapped tightly around her neck, trying to convince the blood to go back into her body through the wide slit in her throat. The woman slumped to the ground, her hands falling from her neck. Standing over her, Jessica was almost proud of how smooth and clean the cut was. It really was a top-quality knife.

Jessica lifted her gaze to face Karen, standing frozen in shock. Karen's mouth hung open and she was still staring at the dead woman on the ground.

"Oh, *now* you don't have anything to say?" Jessica walked toward the other woman. "What's wrong? You had plenty of shit to talk about earlier." She grabbed Karen by the hair and pulled her toward a thick section of limbs and leaves.

Karen came to life, thrashing and kicking at Jessica as she pushed her to the ground.

"What are you gonna do? Tell me how to do my job again? Well guess what, I'll fucking figure this one out, okay? How about I only shoot y'all from here," Jessica plunged the knife into Karen's abdomen, a few inches above her waistline, "to here." She dragged the knife upward.

Karen took a deep breath.

"Oh no you don't." Jessica put a hand over Karen's mouth before she could scream. She leaned in close to whisper in Karen's ear, "I'm sick of people like you." She leaned back, leaving one hand over Karen's mouth and gripping the knife with the other. Jessica pulled it from Karen's chest and shoved the tip into the soft flesh beneath her jaw. Jessica leaned forward, putting all her weight into it as she jammed the knife up and into Karen's skull.

Karen's cheap perfume wafted around Jessica, and she jerked back, pulling the knife free before coughing. "You smell like my grandmother."

She wiped the blade on the grass, folded it up, and shoved it back into her pocket before dragging Bethany over to Karen's side. Jessica picked up Karen's arm and shoved it behind Bethany in a forced embrace. She stepped back, lifted her camera to her eye, and said, "Smile," before taking a few pictures. All from the waist up, of course.

Jessica glanced around the wide tree trunk to see Debbie and her wife still arguing by the fence at the edge of the property. She took off toward the driveway.

Stevie was already heading her way, and in just a few more steps, he would see the women dead on the ground.

"Hey, we decided to take some over by the barn instead," Jessica grabbed the boy's arm and turned him around. "Can you meet us over there? You can just set that stuff right here if you want, I'll get it later."

"Whatever."

The boy dropped the bag at her feet with a clatter, tossed her the car keys, and headed toward the barn. He pulled out his phone as he walked and kept his head down. On the way he passed Douglas, still chain-smoking between the two cars. They nodded at each other, neither caring what the other was doing. Karen's husband didn't notice Jessica walking toward him.

"Hey, Douglas, is it?"

He looked up from his phone and took another drag on his cigarette before blowing the smoke out in front of Jessica.

"Yep."

"How do you put up with that woman?"

His eyebrows furrowed, unsure how to respond.

"Karen. She's such a *bitch*." Jessica stepped closer. "Can I have a drag?"

Douglas stared at her in disbelief.

"Look, this has been real fun, but I have places to be." Jessica grabbed the camera at her side and dropped her shoulder, releasing the strap from her arm. It was hefty, an old Canon 7D with an attached battery pack. She preferred using the battery packs for the vertical grip and manual controls when shooting portraits. Her hand tightened on the grip and swung until the camera struck the side of Douglas' head.

He stumbled against her car before standing back up and lunging toward Jessica. She hit him again. And again. And a few more times just for good measure. The Canon 7D could pack a punch, though she would never use it again for photos. The lens had broken off and fallen to the ground beside him. Blood covered the camera, dripping down onto the mirror inside through the broken lens mount.

Jessica tossed the camera down beside him and picked up the blood-splattered cigarette butt.

"Asshole. That was my favorite lens." She took a long drag on the cigarette and then flicked it onto Douglas' lap.

She lifted the camera around her neck and took a photo of the man slumped against her tire. A headshot, up close and personal. His face, dented and bloodied, filled the screen; framed perfectly by the blood and brain splatter on her car behind him. It really told a story, she figured. That was important, to have your images convey more than just a single moment in time.

Jessica tugged on his jeans and pulled his car keys from his pocket.

Typically, when the clients were on time and didn't irritate the living shit out of her, Jessica would then proceed to the wrap-around porch of the owner's home. Every few feet there would be some blinged-out bench, country sign, or metal artwork. She hardly ever used any of that, sticking instead to the steps leading up to the front of the home. That was one thing Pam had done right. Ten feet across at the bottom, the steps tapered up to the five-foot-wide top step. Vines covered the handrails leading up to the porch and two large columns went from porch to ceiling. It was Jessica's favorite spot on the entire property, but that day there wouldn't be time for pictures on the steps.

Following that spot, she would then take clients around the rest of the porch, wrapping around the house until they were in the backyard. From there, it was a short walk to the barn, a pasture with more trees, and a few horses.

When Jessica turned the corner, Stevie came into view. He was walking back from the barn and had already made it halfway back to the house.

When he noticed Jessica, he raised his hands. "No one was at the barn, I thought we were taking pictures there?"

The little fucker waited long enough, was probably jacking off or on his phone. Or both, who the hell knew? It was all to her benefit anyway, she supposed. Otherwise, she would have had to deal with him before she was ready.

"Yeah!" Jessica walked toward him. "Your mom wanted me to get a few of you by yourself."

Stevie stopped to wait for her, irritated. "I wish she would make up her mind."

She laughed and said, "*Same*, dude."

They walked the rest of the way to the barn in silence.

Next to the barn sat a straw-filled manger with a removable plastic baby Jesus doll. Painted on the side of the barn just behind it was a life-sized mural of Mary, Joseph, the three Wise Men, and a few barnyard animals to round it off. It was quite the hot spot during the holidays. You could replace the plastic Jesus with your very own live baby. Jessica rolled her eyes as she walked by the setup.

"Over here," She gestured to Stevie as they approached a large bale of hay in front of a barbed-wire fence. Stuck in the hay was a wooden sign with "God Bless Texas" painted on it in alternating red, white, and blue paint.

"Man, this is so stupid," he complained.

"Well, there's no going back now. Sit." She pointed to the hay.

Stevie slouched onto the bale, immediately pulling his phone out and swiping up. His eyes never left the screen as he muttered, "Can we hurry? I'm bored."

Jessica looked down at the remaining camera slung around her neck. There was no way she was fucking up her last camera.

"Here, you have something in your hair. Let me just get it. Hold still." She stood over the boy and placed her hands on his head.

"Whatever."

"Little shit," she muttered to herself.

"What?" His eyes remained on his phone.

Jessica's hands tightened around his head, and she pushed backward. He fell off the edge of the hay bale and into the barbed wire fencing behind it. Before he could get to his feet, she shoved the front of his neck onto the barbed wire and sawed from side to side. Blood splattered onto her face and shirt as the sharp barbs tore through his throat like a hot knife through hogs-head cheese. He was younger than the others, though, and quicker to fight back. He managed to push her off him and get to his feet before she pulled out the knife, swinging it in a wide arc until it sliced into the side of his face. But it was too late. The fight drained from him along with the blood pouring from his neck, and he collapsed onto the grass.

Jessica wiped the knife blade on a clean section of Stevie's shirt, put it back in her pocket, and lifted her camera. But something was missing.

She picked up his phone from where it had fallen onto the hay, grabbed a handful of his hair enough to lift his chin, and shoved the cell phone into the ragged slit in his neck. His head lolled backward, but Jessica caught it and pulled it back down onto the phone. A small beep emitted from the depths of his skin as he received a text message.

She took a picture, another headshot. They really were her favorite. If the head was angled just a little toward the sky, you could capture the eyes so vividly. Well, not in his case, but usually.

A scream pierced the air.

She had forgotten about Debbie and her wife. She'd bet the farm that they were getting a good look at Karen and her cousin right about then. Took them long enough.

Jessica ran around the backside of the barn, taking a shortcut to the garden. Out of breath, she stopped to peek around the trunk of an Oak tree. Debbie was sobbing as she shook her mother's body. Her wife stood behind her, frozen with eyes wide and mouth hanging open, her phone still in her hand.

Debbie grabbed her wife's phone and dialed.

"Shit," Jessica whispered, "Shit. *Shit.*"

She bolted around the tree, took a deep breath, and yelled at the women as she ran toward them. "There was a man! Oh my god did you call 911? He ran off that way!" She pointed down the long driveway.

The women spun around to face Jessica, their eyes darting between the blood on her face and the blood on her shirt.

Debbie hesitated a second before dropping the phone and screaming, "We need to get out of here! He could come back."

She jerked her wife's arm and pulled her as they both ran to the car.

Jessica reached into her pocket, pulled the keys she had swiped from Douglas, and hit the lock button.

The two women pulled on the door handles.

"The keys! Dad had the keys. Wait, where is dad? Oh my god, where is Stevie?" Debbie sobbed.

Jessica caught up to them, "They must have gone in the house to call for help."

The three women bounded up the side steps to the porch. As Debbie turned the corner to the front of the house, Jessica grabbed her wife from behind, slit her throat with the pocketknife before she could scream, and dropped her down the steps. As her body tumbled, each bang against the wood was like thunder from a summer storm.

"Baby?" Debbie called out from around the corner.

She ran back to the spot where she last saw her wife, and then screamed at the carnage in front of her. The woman she loved was splayed out at the bottom of the steps, blood covering her throat and dripping down onto her fitted suit jacket and bright yellow tank top. Debbie didn't seem to notice as Jessica came around behind her from the other side of the house. Jessica stabbed her in the back and Debbie tumbled down the steps, landing on top of her dead wife before Jessica could pull the knife back out. Debbie scrambled to simultaneously get to her feet and pull the knife from her back, but her hands fell onto her wife's bloody throat, slipping in the wet blood. Jessica pushed her off the other woman and pinned her face down against the rocks. She jerked the knife from Debbie's back and plunged it back in, repeating the motion until the woman beneath her had stopped screaming.

It was a good thing Pam told her she and the family would be off to church for a special Sunday night service. There was no one to hear the screams. Praise the Lord.

Jessica rolled Debbie over to face her and the woman coughed. The bitch was still alive. Debbie's eyes fluttered open, widening as she saw Jessica lean down close to her face. Jessica brought the bloody knife up close to Debbie's eyes, letting the other woman take a good long look at the sharp edge of the blade before plunging it into her right eye. Jessica felt the slight resistance, then sudden give, as Debbie's eye popped around the knife.

Debbie gurgled, spitting blood onto Jessica's face as she tried to breathe. Jessica jerked back in disgust, dropping the knife onto the driveway where it clattered among the rocks. She wiped her face with her sleeve and picked it back up, reminding herself to sharpen it later, those rocks could really take a toll on a blade. When she turned back to Debbie, the woman was no longer breathing.

Jessica pushed Debbie closer to her wife's body before standing back and staring at the couple. The framing had to be just right. Composition and lighting were the two main things that divided the amateur from the professional. You had to fill the frame, with no empty space above their heads. And if you wanted a unique shot, you needed a unique perspective, an angle most other people didn't get. Jessica stood directly above the women, straddling them as she leaned over for the bird's-eye view she was aiming for. A few shots later, she pulled the camera from her neck, opened her car, and tossed it in the back.

Jessica jumped into the driver's seat and shoved the car into reverse. Without the car's wheel to prop him up, Douglas tumbled down onto the driveway. She put the car back into drive and bumped over the edge of his head, reversing and going back and forth a few times just to be sure.

The old Corolla then lurched forward and barreled down the driveway, crunching over rocks and dust as Jessica headed away from The Smiling Oaks. As she turned onto the highway, sirens echoed in the distance. For once, Jessica was grateful the location was so far out in the sticks. There was something to be said for country living.

Jessica turned the radio up, put on her sunglasses, and headed for the Mexican border. Looked like she wasn't going to make that date. She shouldn't have shaved her legs, after all.

Trash Bags

A black plastic trash bag sits in the
front yard
snatched by a stump.
Winter left it a shriveled, sharp-edged
mess.
The stump, not the bag.
And I wonder if there is a dead baby
inside
born in a bathroom stall or in a home
tossed out like a sticky condom.
I can't look at that Schroedinger's bag
that does and does not contain a dead
baby.
I nudge it with my toe but
there are no dead baby-shaped bits
only the empty bag, ballooned out
by the wind.
I toss it in the bin and
wash my hands and
wonder

why wind looks like dead babies

and trash bags look like

empty wombs.

Those Goddamn Strawberries

Twelve Hours. That's how long it took them to find my body. While there's something to be said for a dating experiment that keeps everyone separated so they can't see each other as they converse, it definitely hindered the discovery of my corpse. You know what, I'm not even mad about it anymore. I was, in the beginning. I'd say I was pretty pissed off. But I'm getting ahead of myself.

It all started with a strawberry.

The day before, as I was getting to know Shawn through the thin wall between us, he mentioned sending over something to celebrate. Of course, I was ecstatic. A celebration meant something exciting was going to happen, and I'd been hoping for a proposal from him all week. You see, we couldn't see each other until we were married. I know... I *know*. Sounds ridiculous. And maybe it was if you were used to finding love in the traditional ways. But I was sick of that. Sick of being pre-judged by my looks, sick of going after guys who were always wrong for me. But Shawn. Oh, he was all kinds of *right*. Sultry, sexy voice. Self-proclaimed mamma's boy, who had lunch with his mom and grandma every Sunday after church. Successful entrepreneur. Home-owner. He even had a dog named Maggie. Who wouldn't love all of that? So yeah, I fell in love with the perfect bastard.

I had just settled onto the couch, kicked my shoes off, and tucked my legs up beneath me. There was a table there, which wasn't unusual. We often had snacks or drinks or whatever we asked for. The company was pretty accommodating with all of that. That day, there was an open bottle of champagne and a bowl of strawberries sitting on the table. I picked up the gold glass next to the bottle. Behind it, hidden until then, was a small black box. *That* was unusual.

I felt like throwing up, and I mean that in the most glorious way imaginable. Shawn was *the* man. The one I was going to spend the rest of my life with, and the one seemingly within minutes of proposing marriage. I hadn't eaten all day, so I popped a strawberry into my mouth, hoping to settle the rolling in my stomach.

On the other side of the wall, a door opened, and footsteps padded against the thick carpet.

"Hey, beautiful."

Oh, that voice. I could have woken up to that voice saying that exact thing for the rest of my life.

"Hey, you," I answered after swallowing, then reached for another strawberry. The butterflies in my stomach were manic.

"Did you get something special over there?"

"I *did*." I smiled, and the strawberry slid down my tongue and slipped to the back of my throat.

"So, I want you to step up to the wall as close as you can get," Shawn purred from the other room.

The strawberry had stuck. I grabbed at my throat but couldn't speak, scream, or let anyone know I needed help. All I could compose was a high-pitched moan.

"I know, baby. I *know*. I'm excited, too."

Oh my god, how could he be so perfect yet so dense? I banged on the wall with my fists.

"I know. We have a lot to celebrate. But first, I want you to know that I'm getting down on one knee."

I dropped to the soft carpet, my eyes bulging. My fingertips fell away from my throat, leaving red scratches where I had tried to claw my way to at least one tiny breath.

"Evelyn, these past few days have been the most wonderful of my life, and I can't wait to spend the rest of my days with you. Evelyn Monroe Richardson, will you be my wife?"

While he was waiting for my answer, I had slipped out of my skin and was somehow hovering over my own body. I screamed, but nothing penetrated the awkward silence.

"Evelyn?"

I yelled and pounded on the wall. When I turned and tried to go to the door, it was like crawling beneath water. I couldn't figure out how to make that new body move the way I needed it to move.

"Evelyn?" Shawn cleared his throat.

Tears flowed down my face as I stared at that wall between us and realized he would never hear me accept his proposal. We wouldn't see each other and fall in love all over again. We would never walk down the aisle, or have kids, or any of the other things we had talked about doing together. It was all so fucking *unfair*.

"Evelyn? Did I misread something? I thought... I thought, well... I thought you would be *happy* about this."

I screamed again, but I may as well have been asleep. Finally able to move, I flew around the room in a rage. The champagne bottle fell to the floor, spilling onto the carpet in a growing dark mass. Strawberries rolled next to it. Those goddamn strawberries.

"Evelyn…" Shawn's voice sounded hard. I had never known him to get angry about anything. Granted, I had only known him a few days, but I *knew* him, you know?

"Evelyn. Well… I guess you don't feel the same way?" Footsteps shuffled on the other side of the wall, and his voice faded. "I can't do this. I can't be here right now." He opened the door, walked through it, and slammed it shut behind him.

About thirty minutes later, Patrick came into the room. By that time, I had stopped screaming and throwing things. When I tried to leave, my hand slipped through the doorknob and disappeared. I was forced to stay there as he tried to talk to me, grew frustrated, and also left. Patrick was okay. He was almost *the* one. But I felt like Shawn was better looking. You know how you can just tell that about a person? You can. Trust me.

No one else came the rest of the day. I hadn't really connected with any of the others, and I'm sure they were off conducting their own proposals.

I had popped that strawberry in my mouth around noon, and it wasn't until midnight when I finally heard the door open behind me.

Kate, one of the staffers, screamed. I watched from the corner as she called others to come, as they called an ambulance, as the ambulance crew tried to revive me, and finally as they carried my body away. It was only then that I could leave the room. *Twelve hours* later.

I floated toward the men's quarters, eager to get a look at Shawn, hoping he was as good-looking as I thought he would be. I mean, yeah, so I was a ghost or whatever. Didn't mean I couldn't *look*.

Her Mother's Smile

"Yogi doesn't like Earl Grey."

"Oh, I'm so sorry, how could I forget?"

The teapot dangles from my fingers over a delicate porcelain cup. Propped in the chair behind it sits Yogi, a stuffed bear who has seen better days.

"I do apologize, Mr. Yogi."

Camilla giggles, her blue eyes twinkling. She has no idea her life is about to be flipped upside down. For that, I am sorry. But *only* that.

I move on to the next cup, behind which sits a duck whose bright yellow feathers and smooth button eyes have yet to age. I glance at Camilla, eyebrows raised.

Her mother's smile beams back at me. There is no doubt Camilla will grow up to be just as beautiful as Katherine was. She clears her throat, resuming the authoritative air of a woman in charge of a very serious tea party.

"Oh yes, daddy. Henry *loves* Earl Grey!"

Water pours from the teapot into the cup, splashing over the sides and wetting the lace table setting beneath. This goes unnoticed by Camilla, her attention already stolen by her own empty cup.

She squirms in her seat and claps her hands.

But for the smile, they are different as night and day. Camilla would never have fallen in love with her coworker. She wouldn't try to leave her husband and child, breaking up a happy home. This sweet girl is nothing like that bitch.

She gulps the "tea" from her cup and offers it up again. This will probably be the last tea party for a long while. I cherish every minute of it, the calm before the storm.

"You're thirsty today, Princess Camilla!"

Suppressing a giggle, she holds her cup steady while I fill it again.

We've already gone around the table at least three times this afternoon. I always "forget" that Yogi despises Earl Grey, wait for her permission to serve Henry, pour her two full cups, and pretend to sip my own.

"When is Mommy coming?"

"In a little bit; she's just resting."

Katherine is upstairs in our queen-sized bed. When I left her, small white bubbles of foam had formed at her lips and her blank eyes stared at the ceiling. The air was thick with promises broken. I had already served her tea, laced with a special ingredient from the clear jar in my briefcase.

I couldn't just let her leave, embarrassing me with her scandalous affair and relegating my time with Camilla to every other weekend. Still not sure what to do with her body, my mind reels through the options as we play at tea.

Camilla laughs.

Distracted, I glance at her across the table, "What's so funny, love?"

"It's *your* tea, Daddy! And you're not even drinking it!"

My eyes follow hers to the floor of her closet and the cup in my hand crashes to the floor.

Sitting on the plush pink carpet is my briefcase, the top flap unlatched. Next to it, the clear bottle...now empty.

I leap across the table to knock Camilla's cup from her hand, but I am too late. Foam bubbles tease at the corners of her mouth, and she is no longer smiling.

Two Months Too Long

My Baby 4-Ever >
Today 2:34 PM

Hello, I hope you are doing well. I know you said not to call you again, but I was wondering if we could get together and talk about all of this. Maybe over dinner? We could go to Umi Sushi. Where we had our 1ˢᵗ date? My treat!

I don't think that's a good idea

Please? I just need to talk to you face-to-face. Tell me what I did wrong so I can work on it. I still love you, baby. I know you still love me. What did I do wrong?

Are you serious? You're doing it right now

Doing what?

Honestly?

Yes, what am I doing that's so wrong? What is SO BAD that you can't even pick up the phone?

You're obsessed. You call me all the time, sometimes 20 times in a row. Even when I tell you that I'll be busy. This isn't normal, Shonda. Like, you have to see that. You don't have any other friends and don't do anything else outside of what we do. You're suffocating me I've told you this a thousand times. Now please stop texting me.

Well, I wouldn't have to if you would just agree to meet me.

Please stop.

Alex's Friend Bradley >
Today 2:55 PM

Hi Bradley. It's me, Shonda. I'm hoping you can do me a favor.

What do you want?

I just need you to have Alex call me, please.

Nope. I'm staying out of that.

Oh, come on, it's just 1 phone call. I would call him, but he must
have blocked me accidentally.

Please don't text me, this is between you and Alex.

Look, you owe me. I never told Alex about that time you grabbed
my ass at the Christmas party.

What? I never grabbed your ass.

Whatever, I'm telling Alex

Good luck getting a hold of him, lol.

Fuck you

———————————

Alex794

Alex, I'm sorry to message you on Twitter but I can't seem to get
a hold of you. Could you please call me? I need to know what

time you want to meet me at Umi Sushi.
3:10 PM

No, please just stop
Alex 794 - 3:28 PM

Stop what? I thought we were going to have dinner and talk
about all of this. Don't you love me anymore? Come on, Alex.
Just meet me so we can talk about this.
3:28 PM

No
Alex 794 - 3:35 PM

____

Alex_794
3:40 PM

Look, Alex. Now you're just being rude. I don't understand
why you won't meet me face-to-face like a real man. First, you

*blocked my phone number, then blocked me on Twitter, now
making me message you on IG like some side piece.*

I said I was sorry, okay?

*You're supposed to forgive and move on. I'm working on things
over here, but how are you supposed to see that if you never talk
to me?*

Answer me, goddamnit

*What, are you with that bitch, Amy? I knew you were cheating
on me. Fuck you.*

*I'm sorry, I didn't mean that. I had a few drinks, you know
how I can get, lol. Please call me.*

Alex

Alex

ALEX

CALL ME NOW

GODDAMNIT, ALEX. I'M NOT PLAYING AROUND HERE. THIS IS SERIOUS. CALL ME. I NEED TO TALK TO YOU.

I'M COMING OVER

I'M HERE, ANSWER YOUR DOOR

ALEX

ALEX

ANSWER THE GODDAMN DOOR

I KNOW YOU CAN HEAR ME I SEE YOUR TRUCK IN THE FUCKING DRIVEWAY

OH YOU CALLED THE COPS ON ME? WHAT A FUCKING LOSER, CAN'T TAKE A JOKE? FUCK YOU

WAIT I DIDN'T MEAN THAT

JUST CALL ME

ALEX

I LOVE YOU, ALEX

5:32 PM

*This is fucking bullshit, and you know it. You can't just ignore
me, Alex. You can't just BLOCK ME everywhere. I deserve
better than this. You can't just break up with me after THREE
MONTHS of dating and not give me an explanation. You owe
me that much, at least.*

Please

I don't owe you anything you crazy bitch. I'm just sorry it
took me two months to see it. STOP MESSAGING ME ON
FACEBOOK. JUST STOP.

———————————

5:45 PM

*Hi Suzanne. This is Shonda. We never met, but we should
have. I'm the girl in love with your son, and he loves me back.
We're just going through a little something right now. You
know how couples can get, you have the good times and the bad*

times. We're in a little disagreement right now, but it's only because Alex won't talk to me to let me clear it up.

You see, I was going through a few things mentally and with my new job and everything. Stress can add up quick, you know? You know how it is, being a woman in a man's world. Always having to prove yourself at work, trying to bust through that glass ceiling, am I right? Anyway, so I had a few bad days where I was a little more emotional than usual, and Alex said he wanted to break up. I know he didn't mean it. I've been nothing but good to him. Seriously, no one will ever love him as much as I do. Sorry to say, not even you. That's how much I love him and how much I'm willing to change for him. I can be whatever he needs me to be. Please tell him to call me. Please.

Sorry to meet you this way, maybe we can have lunch sometime?

———————————————

Mom>

Today 6:19 PM

Alex Wayne, what the hell is going on? Who is Shonda?

What? What are you talking about?

Some girl named Shonda messaged me on Facebook asking me to ask you to call her. Who does that? You are 19 years old. Get your shit together and handle this.

Mom, I swear I'm trying to. She won't leave me alone. We dated for just a few months, and she was crazy since the beginning but...I mean she's really pretty so...well...

Jesus Christ, I thought I raised you better than this. This is how you end up on Jerry Springer, Alex. Leave the crazy ones alone, no matter how hot they are.

I know, I'm trying to. But she won't stop. Just block her, ok?

How do I do that?

Go to her profile and click those three little dots, then select "Block"

How do I go to her profile?

Mom...

What?

I'll just do it for you when I get home later.

Okay well, what am I supposed to do with this until then?

Ignore her.

Fine. Can you stop and get toilet paper on your way home? And remember, it's your night to do the dishes.

Yes ma'am.

From: Rodriguez, Julio (JR)
Sent: Friday, August 27, 2021 10:00 AM
To: <<*SE_TX_Emp_ALL*>>
Subject: PERSONAL BUSINESS AT WORK

ATTENTION ALL EMPLOYEES AT THE SOUTH-EAST TEXAS FACILITY:

Please do not conduct personal business while on company time. We understand life can get in the way, and we are a family-friendly company, but we highly discourage your significant others and/or friends from showing up here. This is a sterile work environment, and we simply cannot have people running past the guard and attempting to get into the factory.

If you have any questions, please email human resources.

Regards,

Julio Rodriguez
Regional Manager / Polis-Marks Foods

———————————

From: Hightower, Alex (AH)
Sent: Friday, August 27, 2021 1:13 PM
To: Rodriguez, Julio (JR)
Subject: Re: PERSONAL BUSINESS AT WORK

I'm so sorry, this will not happen again. I'm considering filing a restraining order against her and can promise you she will not show up here again.

Regards,

Alex Hightower

Packaging / Polis-Marks Foods

———————————

YOU FILED A RESTRAINING
ORDER AGAINST ME?? YOU
FUCKING LUNATIC. I CANNOT
BELIEVE YOU ARE ACTING LIKE
THIS. WHAT ABOUT ALL THAT
SHIT YOU USED TO TELL ME??
LIKE HOW BEAUTIFUL I WAS,
AND THE BEST YOU EVER HAD.
AND YOU'RE WILLING TO THROW
ALL THAT AWAY?? I GUESS
YOU DIDN'T MEAN ANY OF IT. I
GUESS YOU AREN'T THE PERSON
I THOUGHT YOU WERE. I GUESS
I'M STUCK COMMUNICATING
WITH YOU VIA NOTES TAPED

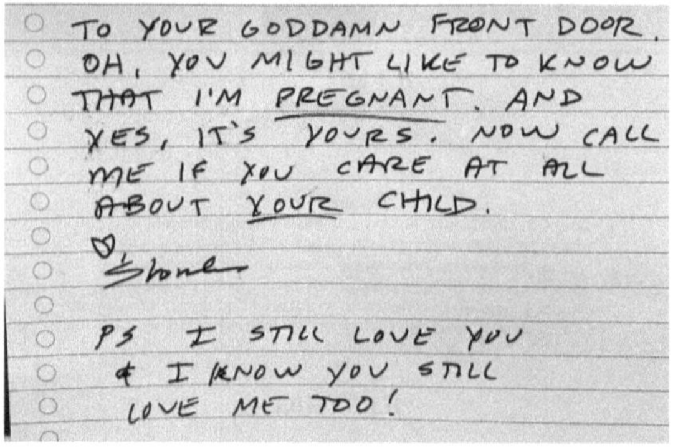

From: Hightower, Alex

Sent: Saturday, August 28, 2021 7:42 PM

To: Ellison, Shonda

Subject: YOU CRAZY BITCH

I am not going to call you, the police recommended I keep our communications in writing only so I have proof of everything. You're now claiming to be pregnant? I'm sorry, but I have a hard time believing that. We used protection every time we had sex. And now that I won't call you back, all of a sudden, you're pregnant? I'm not believing shit until I see a paternity test. GTFO with that bullshit.

-Alex

From: Ellison, Shonda
Sent: Saturday, August 28, 2021 7:45 PM
To: Hightower, Alex
Subject: Re: YOU CRAZY BITCH

Oh, you don't believe me? Are you saying I fucked some other guy? Because I would never do that to you, Alex. You know how much I love you. You're the only guy for me. This IS your baby. Your little boy or girl. Can you imagine it? A little boy with your dark hair and my blue eyes? He'd be a little heartbreaker! What do you think of the name Alex Jr. if it's a boy and Alexa if it's a girl?

Love you forever,

Shonda

From: Hightower, Alex
Sent: Saturday, August 28, 2021 8:29 PM
To: Ellison, Shonda
Subject: Re: Re: YOU CRAZY BITCH

Shonda,

I will not entertain baby names, or any other future plans until I see a paternity test. And, since that probably won't happen until you give birth (IF you actually give birth), I will see you in 9 months.

-Alex

From: Ellison, Shonda
Sent: Saturday, August 28, 2021 8:33 PM
To: Hightower, Alex
Subject: Re: Re: Re: YOU CRAZY BITCH

Future plans? I knew we could work things out. I would love to see you to talk about our future plans. I'll come over tomorrow.

Love you forever,

Shonda

From: Hightower, Alex
Sent: Sunday, August 29, 2021 10:02 AM
To: Ellison, Shonda
Subject: Re: Re: Re: Re: YOU CRAZY BITCH

What? NO, do NOT come over. Again, I will see you when I see a paternity test. Have you even gone to a Dr. to verify this or are you just assuming you're pregnant because your period is a day late?

-Alex

———————————————

From: Ellison, Shonda
Sent: Sunday, August 29, 2021 10:05 AM
To: Hightower, Alex
Subject: Re: Re: Re: Re: Re: YOU CRAZY BITCH

FINE. I won't come over yet. But I just needed to tell you that I'm going to the Dr. next Tuesday. You can't come, they'll only let me go in myself because of Covid. But don't worry, I'll get a nice ultrasound picture for you.

Love you forever,

Shonda

———————————————

From: Hightower, Alex

Sent: Sunday, August 29, 2021 5:33 PM

To: Ellison, Shonda

Subject: Re: Re: Re: Re: Re: Re: YOU CRAZY BITCH

Sure you will.

-Alex

ROSHARON COUNTY SHERIFF'S OFFICE INCIDENT REPORT

INFORMATION ABOUT PERSON INVOLVED IN THE INCIDENT
Full Name: Wayland Center for Women's Services
Home Address: 932 Hyland Street, Suite 860, Marcum, TX

INFORMATION ABOUT THE INCIDENT	
Date of Incident: 08/31/2021	**Time:** 01:16 AM

Location of Incident: 932 Hyland Street, Suite 860, Marcum, TX

Description of Incident (what happened, how it happened, factors leading to the event, etc.) Be as specific as possible (attached additional sheets if necessary)

At approximately 01:16 AM on the morning of 08/31/2021, the burglary alarms at the incident address sounded, and the alarm company alerted the owner, Mark Tartsfield, at his residence. Officers Blakely and Jefferson arrived on scene at 01:38 AM and found the back door to the alley open and a side window broken. Once Mr. Tartsfield arrived on scene with Dr. Patel, it was determined that the only thing tampered with seemed to be the biomedical waste disposal area. Several bags of abortion by-products missing. Pending further investigation.

Were there any witnesses to the incident? NO

If yes, attach separate sheet with names, addresses, and phone numbers.

Was the individual injured? If so, describe the injury (laceration, sprain, etc.), the part of body injured, and any other information known about the resulting injury (ies).

UNKNOWN

Was medical treatment provided?   NO

If yes, where was treatment provided:

REPORTER INFORMATION
Individual Submitting Report (print name):   Elizabeth Jefferson
Signature: *Elizabeth Jefferson*
Date Report Completed: 08/31/2021

From: Ellison, Shonda

Sent: Tuesday, August 31, 2021 9:00 AM

To: Hightower, Alex
Subject: Our Child

Just reminding you that I'll be going to the Dr. today for the ultrasound. I will accept your full and sincere apology later today, for doubting the existence of YOUR child.

Love you forever,

Shonda

———————————————

Operator: 911 state your emergency
Caller: Yes, this is Dr. Parker at Parker and Associates Women's Center. I have something (cut out) can an officer come by?
Operator: I'm sorry, sir, you seem to have cut out. What seems to be the problem? Is anyone hurt?
Caller: No, no one is hurt. I don't think so. But my colleague told me to see if you guys could send someone from McLean over. This isn't exactly a criminal issue I don't think but...

Operator: Sir, what happened exactly?

Caller: One of my patients presented with something strange

Operator: "Strange" sir?

Caller: Yes

Operator: And this was....

Caller: I know it sounds crazy, but she came in for an ultrasound to verify a home pregnancy test and-

(background noise)

Caller: Sorry about that. Anyway, she seems to have placed something pretty far up into her vaginal canal. She refused to let me examine her but it smells terrible. She's getting dressed now - can you hurry?

Operator: Sir, this isn't exactly an emergency. Please hang up and call the main line for Mclean Mental Health requests. *(disconnects)*

From: Ellison, Shonda

Sent: Tuesday, August 31, 2021 4:08 PM

To: Hightower, Alex

Subject: Our Child's First Picture

I'm attaching the ultrasound photo from today's visit. Sorry for the blurriness, I had to take a picture of it with my phone and my hand was shaking I'm so excited for our family. Since this clearly changes things, what time would you like to meet at Umi Sushi tonight? We have a lot to discuss.

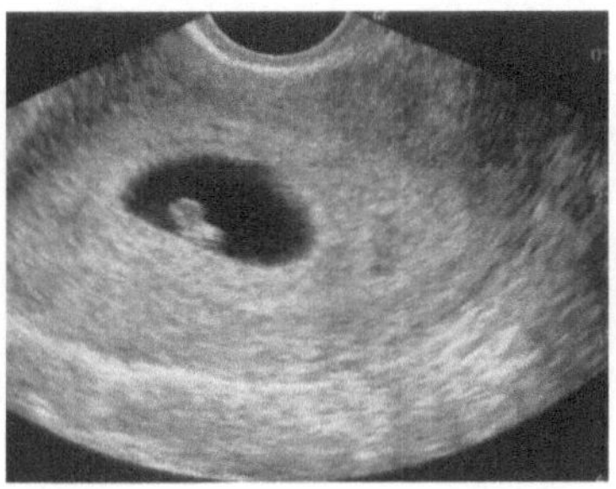

Love you forever,

Shonda

————————————

From: Hightower, Alex
Sent: Tuesday, August 31, 2021 5:48 PM
To: Ellison, Shonda
Subject: Re: Our Child's First Picture

Shonda, I'm not stupid. Obviously, that isn't your photo. I may not be a Dr. but I know they put the dates and names on those things. This is probably from something you found on Google. We WILL NOT be meeting at Umi Sushi later. You're fucking insane.

-Alex

From: Ellison, Shonda
Sent: Tuesday, August 31, 2021 5:50 PM
To: Hightower, Alex
Subject: Re: Re: Our Child's First Picture

ARE YOU FUCKING KIDDING ME? THIS ISN'T GOOD ENOUGH FOR YOU? I'M SO SORRY I WASN'T AWARE OF YOUR MEDICAL DEGREE. I CANNOT BELIEVE YOU ARE STILL DENYING YOUR CHILD. THAT'S FINE I'LL SEE YOU IN COURT YOU PIECE OF SHIT. THANKS FOR NOTHING.

———————————

From: Ellison, Shonda
Sent: Tuesday, August 31, 2021 6:15 PM
To: Hightower, Alex
Subject: Re: Re: Our Child's First Picture

I hope you're happy, all this stress has caused me to miscarry OUR BABY. Since you claim to want "proof" of everything, I'm bringing you OUR DEAD BABY so you can see for yourself what you did to me.

———————————

Operator: 911 state your emergency
Caller: ohmygod ohmygod ohmygod
Operator: Sir, is there an emergency? Where are you?
Caller: I'm at home and...
Operator: What's the address?
Caller: *-redacted for privacy-*
Operator: Do you need an ambulance, sir? Is someone hurt?

Caller: YES, send someone NOW

Operator: Okay sir, I have an ambulance and an officer on the way. Can you tell me what happened? Is there anyone armed? What is your name?

Caller: No...no guns. I'm Alex Hightower. It's my mom...

Operator: Okay, what happened to your mom? Is she hurt?

Caller: Yes. No. I mean, yes, she's hurt. Oh my god, I can't believe she did this.

Operator: Take a deep breath sir – that's it – in....out....in....

Caller: I think my mom is dead

Operator: Okay tell me what you see

Caller: She's on the floor – I just got home – and she's in front of the stairs by our front door and there's so much blood and her phone is next to her and it's broken and covered in blood – ohmygod ohmygod ohmygod

Operator: It's going to be okay, sir. They should be pulling up now. Can you see them?

Caller: Yes I see them outside

(sound of knocking on door)

Operator: Okay I'm going to hang up now, answer your door and get with the officer, please.

(disconnects)

———————————

From: Ellison, Shonda
Sent: Tuesday, August 31, 2021 9:37 PM
To: Hightower, Alex
Subject: I'm Sorry

Look, I'm sorry about your mom. I really am. But you did this to yourself. I didn't mean to hurt her, but you weren't home and she wouldn't call you and let me talk to you. What was I supposed to do, Alex? Huh? You tell ME. WHAT WAS I SUPPOSED TO DO?

P.S. I left a bag for you on the kitchen table. There's your PROOF, DOCTOR Alex

---

The Rosharon Times
Saturday, September 4th, 2021

Obituaries

Shonda Ellison was born on March 19th, 2001 to Bobby and Shari Ellison of Clute, TX. She graduated from Brazoswood High School in May 2020 and lived in the area up until her death. She is preceded in death by her parents, Bobby and Shari Ellison. Shonda passed away on September 2nd, 2021 from an unknown infection. She was found in the alley behind the 1st Baptist Church in Clute by Pastor Muscarella. It is unknown how long she was living there. At this time, no one has come forward identifying as next of kin. Pastor Muscarella has accepted responsibility for her burial.

Donations to the 1st Baptist Church are welcomed.

Fire in the Night

The soft earth shifted as they walked, throwing dust around them like funeral confetti. Abigail pulled on her brother's hand.

"Come on, I'm sure we're close".

Gideon nodded, too tired to raise his eyes to hers. Fallen leaves crinkled beneath their feet, birds yelled at one another across the cloudy sky, and trees rustled in the wind. All a part of the terrestrial symphony around them.

Abigail missed the other sounds: Mama's laugh, Papa's heavy boots on the front porch when he returned home from the fields, the way he would stomp them to loosen the day's dirt and mud before coming into the house. The tea kettle singing from the kitchen.

She didn't miss the crackling of the fire, or her mama's voice calling out to them on that November night. That's what had pulled Abigail from her slumber, her mother's voice. Harsher than usual, high, and frightened.

"Go out the window!"

Abigail had grabbed her brother's shoulders and shaken him awake. She pulled him, sleep-shuffling, toward the bedroom door. The doorknob's hot iron had singed her tender skin, leaving a sizzling ring branded on the pink flesh long after she jerked it back. Beneath the door, in that small space between wood and floor, angry red and orange light flashed. Their mother screamed again, from further away and in between coughs.

"Go out the window!"

So they did. Abigail and Gideon collapsed, coughing, beneath the large oak tree in the front yard. There they remained through the night, tears running rivers down their soot-covered faces while they waited for their parents. Timbers crackled and collapsed, throwing flashing embers up into the dark night. The forest around them held its breath and waited for morning.

The dawn broke with a whisper. Yellow beams of light illuminated dancing plumes of smoke amid the smoldering wreckage. Hesitant at first, the birds resumed their song and the trees their dance while Abigail peered into their parents' bedroom window. Leaning over as far as she dared, her cheeks flushed red with the heat still emanating from what used to be her home.

There was Papa, sprawled out on his back with their mama's favorite butcher knife protruding from his chest, and Mama lying next to him. Abigail jumped back from the window with a gasp.

It didn't make sense. Mama called out to them, why hadn't she left as they did? And the knife... Abigail shook her head and glanced at Gideon behind her, sleeping at the base of the old oak tree. She wiped the tears from her face with the back of her hand, smudging the soot across her cheek, and roused him from his nest of grass and branches. He looked at the house and back up at Abigail, but she couldn't answer the question in his eyes. Not yet anyway. She gathered her arms about him, hoisted him onto her hip, and began walking away from their Mama and Papa and whatever had happened in that room.

They walked in the direction Papa would come when he returned from his trips to town. She hoped they were going the right way.

Liberty Bell

The scratched and worn upholstery irritates the back of her bare thighs. She tugs on the hem of her shorts, trying to cover her pale skin. Jeans would have been preferable, but Greg wanted her in shorts. Said he *loved* her in shorts. She wore them because it was easier than starting an argument.

A silver bell hanging above the doorway waves as people come and go. *Tink-Tink.*

She turns her head, but she knows it is him. She always knows. Like a change in air pressure before a storm rolls, darkness creeps ahead of him. She is the only one who feels it; everyone else only sees light in his bright smile and outwardly affable nature.

Their eyes meet, his boring into hers before she looks away.

She always looks away.

Without a sound he appears behind her, his large hand heavy on the side of her neck, stifling. He bends down and kisses her cheek, talking louder than he needs to.

"Darling, what a great surprise, meeting me for lunch!"

It wasn't a surprise, he told her to be there. Greg always told her where to be.

She manages a smile and avoids his gaze as he slides into the seat across the table from her. Their booth is in a corner, he needn't have bothered with false pleasantries, no one was listening to them. They were all too busy stuffing their faces with greasy burgers, limp french fries, and tepid colas. Staring at their phones instead of talking to one another. How she envies them.

Greg waves to the waitress with a toothy grin and she hustles over, blushing. No one is immune to his charms. The sweet and pungent odor of cheap perfume trails behind her, catching up to their table and engulfing them all in its cloud. She rustles in her apron for her notepad, smiling.

Everyone loves him.

Greg orders for them both. A salad for her, because she had to watch her figure. He *loves* her figure. She despises salads, but it is easier to go along with what he wants.

He rambles about his day, never asking about hers. He didn't have to. She was home, then she was here with him. And what she did at home was no mystery, he watches the security camera feed regularly. He loves knowing she is safe and secure.

His.

Above the door, the bell clangs.

Behind them, a boy begs his mother for ice cream.

On the counter, teapots ring out; shrill, piercing.

A cash register slams shut.

Her chest is heavy, suffocating.

Angela takes a ragged breath and stands up.

He leans back and watches her, amused, "What do you think you're doing?"

She doesn't dare look up; she isn't strong enough. It is taking every bit of willpower she has just to stand. Keeping her head down, Angela turns and hurries out of the diner and away from him.

The bell echoes behind her as she runs.

Flesh Communion

"I've said all this a hundred times. Can't you just read a report or somethin'?"

"I'm sorry, but we need to go through it one more time." A middle-aged man in a cheap suit sat at a wide metal table across from the woman. He leaned toward a dented tape recorder on the table between them and pressed a button. "Please state your name and address for the record."

"My name is Claire Brody. I don't have an address anymore. Y'all kept me locked up for the past six months."

"Mrs. Brody, were you a member of the Branch Davidian Cult living at Mount Carmel in Waco, Texas?"

The woman sighed. "It wasn't a cult, and it was *just outside* Waco, but fine...yes. I was."

"Can you tell me about the events of February 28th, 1993?"

"You should know everything. Y'all were there."

The man reached out and paused the recording. "Mrs. Brody, I need you to cooperate here. For the record." He leaned in closer. "Cooperate, and you'll get to see Jenna."

Claire's eyes narrowed, and she held her breath.

"I'm serious."

"And then we can leave?"

The man tilted his head like he was listening to someone in his ear. He nodded before answering, "Yes, then you can both leave. Go wherever you want. Go back, if that's what you want. I hear some of the crazies are rebuilding."

She wiped the back of her hand across the fresh tears on her cheek and nodded. Once the man hit RECORD again, she straightened up in her chair and spoke. "The morning of February 28th, I was in the chapel with some of the other women. We were halfway through our lessons when it sounded like a car backfired over by the road. Then the window shattered, hurling a hundred pieces of glass into my right arm and shoulder."

The woman grazed her fingers across burn marks on her arm. Somewhere below the angry ridges lay a splatter of glass-shaped scars. Her hand stayed there while her eyes fixed on the two-way mirror at the center of the wall. The twin cassette wheels turned, humming in the silence.

She cleared her throat, turned to face the man, and continued: "I stood by the window, staring at the blood on my arm. It seemed to bubble up in slow motion. All around me, women were running, falling, screaming...but I couldn't hear them. They were just a blur at the side of my vision. Like the swimmy things in the corner of your eyes that disappear when you try to look directly at them. But I didn't look at the people around me. I just stood there, staring at my arm. Enid screamed, so I finally turned around. She was crying and shaking her son Elijah. I'll never forget the way his head just bobbed there against her chest. Limp, like a doll. It was weird, you know? Like everything was happening on the other side of a long tunnel until it all rushed in, pounding me in the chest so I couldn't breathe. It was all so *loud*. I'd never heard such a noise before. The chapel guard shoved me down and took my place near the window, crouching beneath the hole. I jumped up and ran for the door. All I could think about was Brian."

The man glanced at a stack of papers in his hand before asking, "And, for the record, who is Brian?"

"Brian was *everything*."

The man raised his eyebrows and waited for her to continue.

"Do you have kids?" Claire asked him.

He shook his head. "We aren't here to talk about me."

"Of course, you don't. If you did, you'd understand why I did what I did. But you don't, so you won't." She took a sip of water from the small Styrofoam cup on the table in front of her. "Brian is...*was* my son. He was two years old and the most beautiful little boy you ever saw in your life. Looked just like his daddy. That day, he was three doors down from the chapel with a few of the other kids. The Prophet liked to keep families apart as much as possible and said it 'strengthened our reliance on God' or something. I was having my doubts about that long before a bullet came flying through the window. When the Prophet took Jenna—" She stopped, leaned in toward the recorder, and stared at the man as she continued, "my *fourteen-year-old daughter*, as one of His wives, it bothered me. By that time, I'd been one of His wives for about three years. It's not like He'd always kept to His own age. He took brides as young as sixteen before, but never as young as Jenna."

The air-conditioner kicked on with a thump and a rattle above them. The stained ceiling squares shuddered, then settled back down.

"We'll get to that. For now, let's focus on what happened February 28th."

"Yes, yes. Everyone wants to know what happened. I needed to find Brian. I ran down the hallway, and the windows ahead spit out more bullets and glass, but I finally made it to Brian's door.

"The classroom didn't have windows. The Prophet thought it would be too distracting for their young minds to see the world outside when they were supposed to be focusing on His teachings. Young minds wander more since they don't always have the self-control of the older ones. You'd know about that if you had kids. Anyway, they were huddled in a corner of the room without a single adult in sight. Marcia and Penelope were gone, probably off looking for their own kids. I didn't really blame them. Isn't that what I was doing? Though I hadn't abandoned six toddlers to do it. Brian ran up and grabbed my leg with a fierceness I'd never seen from him before. I crouched down to hug him and told him I was there for him, always. That I'd always find him. Then more gunshots rang out. I asked if he could be a big boy for me, then asked him and the other five kids to hold hands and follow me out of the room. They were all quiet. That's weird, for them. I mean it *should* be weird. A child's response to chaos isn't normally quiet obedience."

"This is when you took the kids to the kitchen?" the man asked.

"Yes. I'm getting there. We stayed low against the counters. We heard more gunshots, and then a heavy thumping flew over the building, fading off into the distance. It was a *helicopter*. A helicopter was flying over Mount Carmel. We were under attack, just as the Prophet had predicted."

"What happened next?"

"I could still hear Enid crying from the chapel, and I pulled Brian into my lap and kept my arms around him. That could have been *us*, you know. Anyway, heavy footsteps thundered down the hall and I held a finger to my lips and made eye contact with the two kids on my left, and the three on my right. The steps moved on into the cafeteria and I quietly thanked God for His protection over us. I learned later there wasn't anything to fear. It was just William and Paul, checking on everyone."

"Did you see the Prophet?"

"No. I did wonder where He was at that moment... if He held my Jenna safely in His arms or had left her alone and scared like those women left the little kids. I didn't see Him until later."

"They were checking on everyone...so it was over?"

"They said it was. But it was far from over. You know that. I don't really remember how we got to the common room, but we all stayed there the rest of the night. The whole place was as quiet as the dead. Everyone was too scared to talk. I think we were all in shock. I mean, yeah, we expected to be attacked. We trained for it. But it's different when it's actually happening, you know? No, you wouldn't, would you? Mind if I smoke?" She pulled a pack of cigarettes from a bag at her feet and lit one without waiting for an answer.

Claire exhaled a puff of smoke, then lowered the cigarette. "Oh, I know, I know we're supposed to be *healthy*. Bodies are temples and all that. The whole time I was at Mount Carmel, I never once smoked. Gave it up cold turkey. The Prophet wanted us *pure,* and we always did whatever He wanted. We didn't smoke or drink, and we ate right."

"Weren't you vegetarians?"

"Sure. Well, mostly. Anyway, back to the thing. The shooting stopped. Though that's never been the issue, has it?"

"I'm sorry?"

"It's never been a matter of when the shooting *stopped*, but who *started* it to begin with, right?"

"Who do *you* think started it?"

"Honestly? I don't know for sure. These guys were waitin' for a fight. Both sides. But if I had to put my money on it, I'd say y'all started it, not us. That shot in the window was the first sound I heard, and it came from the outside. Last I checked, we weren't shooting *ourselves*. Didn't really matter, though. It was gonna happen eventually." Claire tapped ashes into the empty cup in front of her.

"Because the Prophet said so?"

"Well, yeah."

"What else did He predict?"

"He knew there would be sacrifices. People were gonna die. And they sure did, didn't they?"

"What happened next?"

"We went on with normal life. Breakfast, teachings. Lunch, teachings. Dinner, teachings. Sleep, repeat. All the time with the teachings. We didn't always eat between them: sometimes He made us fast. But that was just before the special services."

"What happened during the special services?"

"Ohhh, I get it now. That's why I'm here? Y'all want to know more about *that*? I'll tell you anything you wanna know; don't really care anymore. I'm a changed woman...just wanna see Jenna and get out of here." Claire finished her cigarette and tossed the butt into the cup with the ashes.

"So, the *special* services...us women would go down to the basement with the Prophet. The other men were in charge of the kids. Most of 'em, anyway. That was probably the most time they ever spent alone with 'em."

"But in the basement..." he prodded.

"Yeah." Claire paused and looked at the two-way mirror set into the wall.

"There's no judgment here. I'm just trying to get all the facts. What happened in that basement?"

Claire turned back to the table and leaned forward on her elbows. One leg was wobbly, and the table shifted with her weight. "*Flesh Communion,*" she whispered.

"Please speak up," the man said as he gestured toward the recorder.

Claire leaned against the back of her seat and took her arms off the table. It tilted back into place. She glanced at the mirror again, took a deep breath, and said, "Flesh Communion. That's what He called it. You familiar with communion?"

"Yeah, I used to be Catholic."

Claire nodded her head and said, "So you know."

"Well, we didn't exactly…"

"Oh, of course you didn't. No one did. But the Prophet explained it all to us. It was the only way."

"The way to what?"

"To getting closer to the twenty-four. He said if the women took part in the Flesh Communion, God would bless our wombs and we would produce the twenty-four that would rule after the return of Christ."

The man stared at her.

"It's in Revelations. Look it up."

"But the children He used…"

"Were His? Yeah. You think it don't make sense, right? Why take His own kids if the purpose is to have more?"

"Well…*yeah.*"

"We didn't do it all the time. Just every nine months. And He took the weak, the disobedient. Sometimes He'd take them to get back at their mothers for some perceived slight. The Prophet was good at that, finding faults in people. I can see that now. I can see a lot of things now."

The man tilted his head again and stared ahead, unfocused, as he touched his earpiece. He nodded before saying, "Ok, let's stay in order here."

"The suits in your ear want the whole story, then?"

"Let's go back to February 28th. You said you went on with your normal routines?"

"As normal as we could, anyway. The women and kids were told to keep to the schedules. The men didn't."

"What did the men do?"

"Mostly? Talked, argued, tried to figure out what to do about y'all in the front yard."

The man flipped through the notepad in front of him, then said, "A few of the women and children evacuated. Why didn't you leave with your kids then?"

"I could have. *Should* have. Maybe everything would have turned out different." She looked down at her hands clenched tightly in her lap. "The Prophet didn't want any of His kids to leave. And, you know Brian was His child, so he had to stay. Since Jenna was His wife, He wasn't letting her leave either. I *did* try, you know? To get out. I begged Jenna to go with me and Brian. We were gonna climb out the broken chapel windows when no one was looking. But she was too scared. I could have left without her. Could have gotten Brian out. But I thought I could convince her, thought it would be okay until then. I chose to stay there with her, even though we weren't even allowed to see each other. What kind of mother does that? Chooses one child over the other? *Sophie's Choice* is what that is. And it's *my* fault he's dead."

Claire kept staring at her hands in her lap. She twisted her fingers until the burn scars turned white. "But, uh," she said as she cleared her throat and looked back up. "We didn't get to leave."

"Did you ever hear the Prophet talking about His plans?"

"Oh no. They wouldn't let us near all that. Beatrice said they were making some kinda deal, but I guess she was wrong 'cause that's not how things ended." Claire lit another cigarette, took a long drag, and watched the smoke curl upward toward the ceiling.

"Y'all wouldn't let us sleep. Do you know what that does to someone's mind? Of course, you don't. Every night it was noise. Chants, music, animals being slaughtered. Who does that? Was it you? Did you decide what to play all night to keep us awake?"

"No."

"That song, 'These Boots Are Made for Walking', over and over." Claire scratched her ear. "It's permanently crocheted into my ears now. Leaks into my brain at night. You should find out who played that stuff. Maybe give him a head check himself. Keep *him* in a room for six months."

The man sighed and shifted in his chair.

"I heard later it was fifty-one days. You know, during, it felt like ten years and ten seconds all at the same time."

"Did you ever go into the basement again?"

She exhaled, seeming to shrink into her chair before answering, "Yeah, several times. He didn't want to wait nine months in between anymore. Like I said, sleep deprivation makes you act different. He was also shot, but y'all know that already. He got shot that first day. Probably woulda healed fine, if He'd gone to a hospital or somethin'. But it was smelling real bad by the end. Maybe that's why He did it..."

"Tell me about the first time you went there after the shooting happened."

"It was, I don't know, maybe a couple of days after that first shooting. We thought maybe it was gonna happen because we didn't have breakfast. But with everything going on, we weren't sure. We were gettin' kinda low on food by then. I thought maybe they were just rationing. By lunchtime, when there still wasn't food, I knew what was going on."

"Did it usually happen around lunchtime? This 'Flesh Communion'?"

"Oh no. It was always at 3:00 am."

"Why?"

Claire shrugged. "The Prophet said so. He said Jesus died at 3:00 pm, up there on the cross. I mean, we all know that, but He said the Flesh Communion should happen in the mirror time of that. To be closer to God or something. We weren't allowed to question Him."

"Okay, it's 3:00 am. What happens next?"

"Well, about 2:30 am, the guards started waking up all the women. We went down into the basement while the other men and kids slept. Two guards stayed in the kitchen to make sure nobody interrupted."

"And the child that was picked?"

"Oh, we never knew that until afterward, when we went back to our rooms to check on our own kids. You'd always know who it was by who didn't show up for breakfast the next day. The Prophet allowed for a day of mourning for the mother, but no more than that. Anything more, and you were just being dramatic, you know?"

"So, you're going down into the basement with the other women…"

"There was a long table down there, probably could have seated the whole commune. We'd sit down in front of empty white plates. There wasn't any order to the seats or anything. And then we'd wait for the Prophet to enter." Claire leaned back in her seat and looked across the room at the blank wall behind the man. The end of her cigarette turned to ash and hung, waiting.

"He'd come down wearing these white robes. Then, He'd take his seat at the head of the table, and one of the guards would uncover another, smaller table at the back of the room. In the middle of that was a Dutch Oven. Do you know what those are?"

"Yeah."

"Oh. Some men don't. Guess you've done a little cookin'. Anyway, it was an old one, covered in chipped blue paint with white spackled all over it. They would set the whole thing in front of the Prophet."

"He'd eat, too?"

"Are you gonna let me tell this? I'm only doing it once. It's…too much."

"Sorry. Please go on."

"The woman to his right always went first, whoever that was. That first time after the shooting, the time we're talkin' about, it was Margaret. I only know because I was on *her* right. Margaret stood up, picked up her plate, and moved closer to the Prophet. That's when He opened the Dutch Oven. The smell...that's what I remember most. Smelled like my mom's Sunday pot roast. Oh, I see your face. I know that's horrible, but that's the only way I know to describe it. It would be hot, still steaming. For a second, all that steam would hide the Prophet's face. Then it would clear, and He'd smile at us."

She tipped the ashes into the cup.

"Margaret held out her plate, and He sliced off a thin sliver of the meat and placed it there. Then she sat back down, and I was next. This was repeated until every woman had meat on the plate in front of them. Then, He'd place the lid back on and the guard would pick it up and put it on the table in the corner. I never knew what they did with the leftovers. Maybe they fed it to the dogs? They hardly ever got meat. We're vegetarians, you know."

"Yes, you said that. You said you were 'mostly' vegetarians."

"Well, this is the 'mostly' I'm talkin' about now, isn't it?"

"What happened next?"

"He'd read from the Bible."

"You remember the verse?" Before Claire could respond, the man held up his hand, popped the cassette player open, and flipped the tape to the other side. Claire drummed her fingers on the table as she watched him. He shut the recorder with a loud snap and pushed the RECORD button.

"Of course, I do. John 6:53-58. *Jesus said to them, Truly, truly, I say to you, unless you eat the flesh of the Son of Man and drink his blood, you have no life in you. Whoever feeds on my flesh and drinks my blood has eternal life, and I will raise him up on the last day. For my flesh is true food, and my blood is true drink. Whoever feeds on my flesh and drinks my blood abides in me, and I in him. As the living Father sent me, and I live because of the Father, so whoever feeds on me, he also will live because of me."*

"Then?"

"What do you think? We ate."

The man shook his head in disgust, opened his mouth, glanced at the recorder on the table, then closed his mouth again.

"Yeah, I know what you're thinking. But you weren't there, were you? Not inside, anyway. Plenty of you were outside, driving tanks around tryin' to scare us."

"What happened next?"

"We went back upstairs and found out which kid was missing."

"You said it usually happened every nine months, but more during the fifty-one days?"

"Yes."

"How many more times before April 19th?"

"Five. Five more times. We had to use candles later, once y'all cut our power off. But at least it was cooler down there than in the house."

"Do you remember what happened on April 19th?"

"Yes. But the most important thing happened the night before."

"What was that?"

"Our final Flesh Communion." Claire took a deep breath and continued. "Happened just like all the others. Until we went back to our rooms..."

The man watched her.

"... and Brian was missing," Claire choked as tears flowed down her face. "I had eaten..." She sobbed, put her arms on the table, and laid her head in them, burying the rest of the words.

The man stared, then looked toward the window. He couldn't see the men on the other side watching, but they spoke to him again through his earpiece. He cleared his throat.

"Do you know why? Why Brian was chosen?"

She picked her head up and whispered, "Oh yes. I know why." Claire wiped her eyes and stared at the man. "I tried to leave again. *Begged* Jenna to come with us. She said no, that what I was saying was blasphemous and against the will of the Prophet. Then she went back to His room."

"The Prophet's room?"

"Yeah. She told Him. I don't know why. Surely, she wouldn't have if she had known... He turned her against us. It wasn't her; it was always Him. She was just a child herself. He was a very charming man. You've seen His videos?"

The man ignored her question as he asked, "And this was the night before?"

"Yeah. The next morning, since I was allowed to stay in my room for my day of mourning, they left me alone. That's where I was when there were great big rumbling noises, and the whole building shook. Gunfire rang out again, just like that first day."

"You were in your room the whole time?"

"Oh, no. I got Him back."

"Excuse me?"

"I shot Him."

"You shot who?"

"Him. The Prophet. It was loud and everyone was running around. I thought I was gonna die, but I didn't care about that. In the hallway, someone lay face-down under a window. The back of their head was missing, and their gun was on the floor next to them. So, I picked it up."

"You just picked it up? What about the tear gas?"

"Oh yeah, it was bad. I almost didn't make it to Him. But luck was on my side. Who's God watching over *now*, huh? The Prophet was leaning against a wall by the kitchen, mostly dead from his infected wound. But I shot Him in the head, anyway."

"You... *what*?"

"Shot Him. In the head. But you can't blame me. I was under *extreme emotional distress*, you know. And sleep-deprived. But I'd do it again right now if I could. I'd shoot Him a dozen times if I had the chance. He deserved it."

"And where was Jenna during all this?"

Claire looked down at the table and picked up the Styrofoam cup, now filled with ashes and cigarette butts. She turned it around in her hand as she answered, "They told me she got out, and that's when I started the fire."

"*You* started the fire?"

"I did. I wanted Him to burn for what He'd done. And I was okay to burn with Him, just to make sure it was done. Didn't have nothin' to live for anymore. Jenna was safe. Brian was gone..."

"But you got out."

"I'm here, ain't I?" Claire rubbed the burn scars on her arm. "You know, I'll never forget that smell."

"What smell?"

"People burnin'. Smelled just like that Sunday pot roast."

The man leaned forward; eyes narrowed. "There's been zero evidence of this 'Flesh Communion' happening."

"Well, there wouldn't be, would there? The basement collapsed in the fire. We were Branch Davidians, not engineers or carpenters. You ever wonder why there aren't many basements in Texas?"

The man sighed and leaned back in his chair. "No, never thought about it."

"I looked it up one day, after. Not like there was anything else to do while y'all had me locked up. There's loads of reasons. Water tables are too close to the surface, marshy soil is too unstable, and you wouldn't want 'em below sea level down by the coast. And too much flooding with all our rivers and bayous."

"There isn't evidence of this because of water tables?"

"You combine shiftin' ground, unstable basements, and piss-poor structural support and what do you get? An accident waiting to happen. I just helped it along, is all."

"We'd still find bones, though."

"He buried 'em. Never let nobody help. We never knew where they were."

"We're supposed to just take your word for it, is that right? How do I know you're telling me the truth?"

"It happened. I swear on it. You're just gonna have to believe me."

"Why would I believe you?"

"Because I'm a *victim*. I didn't deserve any of this. You think I enjoyed killing Him? Enjoyed *eating my child*?" Claire pulled on her hands harder.

"Yeah, I do, actually. I think you were so deep in that cult; you'd have done anything He asked you to, even putting Him out of His misery there at the end."

Her hands became still as she looked up at him. She studied his face and whispered, "*Prove it.*"

A Werewolf's Lament

Listen to the silence. Engorged on a future that will never be, it permeates the air around you as you kneel at her grave.

It speaks of moonlit walks along the canal, hands clasped tightly.

It speaks of a first kiss, stolen in the shade of the oak tree behind her mother's house.

It screams of a dream's abrupt death.

These moments whirl around you as you crouch in the eye of the silent storm and regret the actions that led you both there. Her, cold and rotting in a cheap wooden casket beneath the ground. You, alone.

She was too good for you, you know this. You've always known this. But somehow, through Cupid's misplaced arrow, she loved you back. You tried to warn her, but she would laugh that beautiful laugh of hers. Her chestnut eyes would light up, and you would forget every reason you had to push her away. Of course, she always thought you were joking. But you never joked about your darkness.

If she had only listened, she would still be alive. Gorgeous Victoria, with skin like fresh milk and hair black as a moonless night. She was beautiful even in death. The most beautiful woman you had ever known.

You managed to beat it for years, locking yourself in a steel cage on nights with a full moon under the guise of working late. But doubt had crept in, and you knew she wasn't buying it anymore. She thought there was another woman... as if you could ever love someone the way you loved her. The truth was much worse than any sordid affair.

She followed you that fateful night, down into the dungeon. You were so obsessed with getting there in time, that you didn't hear her small footsteps behind you. Once inside the cage, you dropped the key in a box by the door that only a human hand could reach into, then sat down among the spider webs to await your fate. How were you to know she was watching from the shadows?

When she appeared, you yelled at her to stay back but she slipped her slender arm through the bars and into that box with the key. Ignoring your pleas, she pulled the key from its hiding place and into the lock hanging from the gate. There were eleven links in the chain and each one hammered a nail into your heart as it clattered to the ground.

You scrambled to put the chain back and close the lock, but your inhuman hands had stopped obeying your human mind. Your fingers dropped the key as long claws protruded from your nails.

You'll never forget the look on her face when you turned toward her with a snarl. Or the way her screams cut off when you ripped into the flesh at her soft throat, and you knew you'd never love another.

The storm of loss rages there, at her grave. And you are silent.

The Bay Sirius Witch of Atchafalaya Basin

Nestled deep in the heart of the Atchafalaya Basin in Louisiana is the Bay Sirius Swamp. At the bottommost edge of Butte La Rose, the Swamp used to be home to Bayou Chene, a thriving logging community. After the flood of 1927, twelve feet of silt covered everything Chene ever was, or would be again. Before that, it was the Village of Bones occupied by the Chitimacha Tribe. No one knows who was there before the Chitimacha, or when the Witch first came to the Swamp.

For generations, Cajun grandmothers passed down legends of the Bay Sirius Witch. Told as a cautionary tale to not stray too deep into the Swamps, the threat had always been an effective one. Young boys and girls would stay close to their mothers when crawfishing, lest the Witch snatch them away. Older children would dip their toes at the edge of her Swamp and dare each other to go find the Witch. It was always an idle threat, a silly game.

Until it wasn't.

It happened in the Summer of 1935 before the sun dipped below the horizon and the air was still thick with the day's heat. Two young girls set off to test their bravery. Agnes Marie and Odette, both twelve years old, pushed out on a homemade raft for the direction of Bay Sirius. Odette's parents thought she was having a sleepover with Agnes Marie, and Agnes Marie's parents thought she was staying with Odette. With lanterns full of oil and hearts full of courage, they pushed off from the muddy banks behind Odette's home.

Agnes Marie was the bossy one of the two and, as such, insisted that Odette be the first to steer them. With a stick as big around as her forearm, Odette guided them through the waterways. She would push the stick deep into the mucky swamp bottom, lean on it to propel them forward, then pull it up with a "schlock" and start all over again. It was tedious work, and Odette was soon tired of it. She was thankful for the setting sun and its implied coolness from the scorching day. Deep in the Swamps, the sun couldn't reach you much anyway. Day or night, it didn't matter. The same dense, wet air clung to your clothes and seeped into your bones.

Excitement soon dwindled to nervousness as they meandered through the swamp, steering their homemade raft around the towering Tupelo trees. The crooked roots twisted from the brackish waters like outstretched arms, lit only by the twin beacons from their lanterns. The flared, moss-covered trunks narrowed as the trees rose in the night sky; majestic giants who ruled the Swamps. A nutria rat glared at the girls from within a tangle of roots at the base of a particularly large tree. It, too, seemed eager to see what would happen to them that night.

The girls kept on their path, steering clear of water moccasins and gators as best as they could. Odette grew more uncomfortable by the minute.

Small waves billowed out in circles around their raft and broke against the tree trunks. Cypress trees mixed in with the Tupelo as they went deeper into the Swamp. The red knobby roots reached out to the girls as if to say, "Stop. Beware." Dark lines on the trunks loomed high above the girls' heads, revealing the depth of the 1927 floodwaters.

Agnes Marie and Odette drifted by the trees, oblivious to their warnings while the swamp rose around them in a chorus. Crickets sang, bats flapped their wings, and crawfish and other creatures splashed in the water.

"Let's just head back," Agnes Marie whispered, her voice quivering.

Odette nodded her agreement, eager to get back to her home. She hadn't wanted to go into the swamp in the first place but couldn't let Agnes Marie think she was a scaredy-cat.

They turned around, rowing faster than when they had first come into the swamp. Holding their breath, they didn't dare speak. Something hung in the air. Something... different, heavy. Something they no longer wanted any part of.

Before they had gone two feet, a large splash echoed behind them and water flew over the girls, washing away any remnants of bravery. A thin scream pierced the night as an unseen force jerked Odette from the back of the raft and into the shadows beyond, violently rocking the small wooden vessel. Agnes Marie flew through the air and into the water, followed by both lanterns. Panicked, she swam as fast as she could toward home. Once there, she fell onto the muddy banks, gasping for breath. With every remaining bit of energy she had, she rose to her feet and ran inland. She did not look back.

Agnes Marie eventually returned to the banks and waited all night for Odette. That's where Agnes Marie's parents found her, right before lunch the next day. Shivering, even though she was dripping with sweat and baking in the late morning sun.

Odette never made it home.

Search parties combed the Swamp for a week before giving up. Every group that came back had bloodshot eyes, trembling hands, and wouldn't talk to anyone for hours. When they did, they spoke of hearing Odette's scream and the clunk of wood, like a raft pushing through the Swamp. The noise would get closer until it felt like someone was breathing on the back of their necks. Then, a loud cackling would pierce their ears, causing them to bend over in pain. They would turn around, yelling, "Who dat!?", but there would be nothing behind them but the tupelo trees.

So it was with the Bay Sirius Witch of Atchafalaya Basin. Sometimes, when the crickets take pause and the wind catches its breath, you can still hear Odette's screams and the soft thud of the raft making its way through the Tupelo trees.

I Watch Them

A young couple spills onto the sidewalk from an all-night diner, laughing and holding hands. Before the door closes, the scent of burgers sizzling on a grill wafts out into the night. As they stop to embrace, a man in a leather jacket sidesteps them, rolling his eyes and muttering beneath his breath.

I watch them kiss.

Young men gather beneath me. They talk of futures, families, and hope, while they wait to cross the street. Car keys jingle in their hands. Two of them graduate next month, and one already has an impressive job offer. The tall, gangly one is starting a charity for the homeless. World-changers, all of them. Or at least they want to be.

I watch them dream.

A woman with a black satchel over her shoulder approaches, the bag bumping against her hip as she walks. Clutching her hand is a young boy with remnants of an after-dinner ice cream still on his chin. She stops in front of the large mailbox cemented to the sidewalk. The boy reaches into the bag and pulls out a package, then the mother leaves the bag at her feet and lifts him up to the bin opening.

I watch them laugh.

They don't see the man in the leather coat behind them. He grabs the satchel at their feet, stuffs it beneath his jacket, and ducks into the diner.

The mother hugs the boy before she sets him back onto the sidewalk beside her and turns to grab her bag.

I watch them cry.

A traffic light changes, the soft click almost drowned out by car engines coughing to life on one side, and brakes squealing on the other. The young couple hurries across the road, still holding hands. An old man, leaning down to adjust his car radio, plows through the intersection.

I watch them fall.

The dreamers beneath me jump into action. One calls the emergency line while another, the impressive-job-offer graduate, kneels to help the couple bleeding out onto the pavement. The tall one directs traffic around them, but it doesn't matter anymore. It's too late. They wait for the ambulance, shoulders drooped and silent. They know they won't be changing anyone's world tonight.

I watch them try.

Horns bleat in the distance as drivers grow impatient with the stalled traffic. Angry men and women roll their windows down and yell at the cars in front of them, shaking their fists into the cold night. Emergency vehicles struggle to find a path forward.

I watch them fail.

My light flickers, as it has for the past two nights. City workers came to fix it yesterday, but they didn't have a spare and aren't allowed to buy any more. Budget cuts, you know. The street below flashes in and out of my vision. A young woman looks up and watches me cycle on ... off ... on, her eyes a delightful shade of green.

I watch-

The Finest French Lace

Jane coughed beneath her nest of furs and quilts by the stove. Tiny and frail, she was barely visible above the layers. She had it, the sickness. Doc Frankum said it wouldn't be long, that most lungers didn't last as long as she had, especially being as young as she was. Mary thought Jane was holding on to see Elizabeth, their eldest sister, married.

That's what Elizabeth was doing that very minute, out by the river. It was where William had first asked for her hand. Their mama said it was romantic, but their daddy had grumbled about having to cart everyone off through the pasture. He said pastures were for the cows and he couldn't understand why anyone would pass up on a nice indoor wedding. Mama won that battle, as she always did.

Everyone agreed Jane shouldn't go out in the winter air. Everyone but Jane, anyway. She had cried, mumbled that she understood, then coughed until she turned blue. Mary volunteered to stay with her. It was the only logical choice. Elizabeth couldn't very well miss her own wedding, and Mama *had* to be there. Mary was sure they would tell her all about it when they returned. It would almost be as if she were there. Almost.

The party set off for the river earlier that afternoon, bundled in their bulky furs and finest wedding clothes. Both the bride and groom's family and Father Caney had squeezed themselves onto two wagons. At the bend in the road, Elizabeth turned and waved, her dress bunched up around her, the lace veil flapping in the wind. Mama bought it all special from a mail-order catalog straight from Paris. Elizabeth had cried when she opened the package. It was the most beautiful thing any of them had ever seen. Decorated with intricate lacework, the long ivory dress was a work of art. The veil repeated the fine lace pattern, so delicate it could be mistaken for a spider's web.

Back in the house, Mary put the kettle on and rearranged Jane's blankets. She leaned down and moved the fine blond hair off her closed eyelids. She was sleeping, finally. She wouldn't stay that way for long before waking with coughing fits enough to soak a handkerchief with blood.

She was the sweetest among them, and it wasn't fair she was being taken so young. Mary sat on the floor next to her sister and watched her sleep, covering her frown with a smile the minute Jane's eyes fluttered open.

"Hey," she whispered.

"Mary...I know. I know I'm lookin' to die." Jane coughed; the top of her blue eyes barely visible above the red-splattered handkerchief clutched to her mouth.

"Hush now, you don't know that." Mary stood up to fetch a glass of water.

A wolf howled in the night, piercing through the cold winter air. Rubbing the goosebumps on her arms, Mary pulled the curtains back on the window to peer outside.

The bunkhouse was barely visible through the pale light of the moon to the right of the road. The building brimmed with cowhands during peak season, and she liked to watch them work the cattle during the day and return, heavy with exhaustion from the day's heat. They'd unsaddle their horses, wipe the sweat from the massive beasts, and leave 'em to the night wranglers before taking care of themselves. She would watch as the lamps, heavy with tallow, flickered in the bunkhouse windows. The scent of sweat, dry cow manure, old leather, and tobacco would carry on the wind toward her home.

But that night, the bunkhouse sat in darkness. Most of the cowhands were long gone. All they had to do in the cold season was work the tallow and hides, so most of the crew headed to town, but for the lucky ones with families to go see. Only two of 'em had stayed on for the winter, a Mexican named Manuel and a white man named Billy. A few of the steers had gone missing earlier that week, so Manuel and Billy had set off before the wedding party to check on the herd.

Mary leaned closer to the glass and squinted. There, on the road leading out to the river, was the largest wolf she had ever seen in her life. Thick gray fur undulated in the wind, but the large beast didn't move. Behind it, there had to be forty more just as big. A chill ran up her spine as she watched them. They seemed to be watching her, though she knew that was impossible. She snapped back from the window.

Jane, reading the panic and confusion on Mary's face, whimpered. The tears that were hovering on the edge of her eyelids spilled over as she lost the small amount of control she was mustering.

"Shh, Janey." Mary pulled her sister into her arms and caressed the top of her thin shoulders. "Everything's fine. They'll be back 'fore you know it."

When Mary turned her eyes back to the road outside, she jumped away from the window and screamed. The wolves had moved closer to the house, and the largest one had stepped onto their porch, yellow eyes boring into hers.

Hanging from one of its sharp teeth and partially stained a dark red, was a shredded scrap of the finest French lace.

Just a Dream

Cold seeped into her skin from the bottom of the steel cage, infecting her bones with a bitterness she couldn't shake. A meager bit of light spilled from a round window high above her. Huddling in the corner, she wrapped her arms around her knees and shivered until the light flickered out, plunging her into darkness.

She held her breath, waiting for it to return. It did that sometimes, she remembered. On. Off. On. Off. Like a great bird flying in front of the sun, or a storm passing by on its way to wreak havoc somewhere. The flashes of light seemed to coincide with the rocking motion of the floor beneath her. That, combined with the stench of feces and mold, sent bile rising to her throat.

She tamped down the nausea, closed her eyes, and remembered a child...

***

From the first moment her swollen belly moved, Ann was hooked. Captivated by the life growing larger beneath her skin, she eagerly awaited the day she could see her child in the flesh. After the baby was born, she often rocked him to sleep in her grandmother's wooden rocker, softened with strategically placed pillows and blankets. There was comfort in knowing that generations of women in her family were rocked to sleep in that chair and had then rocked their own children to sleep. As the wood creaked, she sang a lullaby so intertwined with those generations, that it may as well have been etched into the rocker itself.

She was happy. *They* were happy.

Until the nightmares, anyway.

Her husband, Carl, said it was normal. That it was simply new-mother worries and concerns manifesting into her subconscious. The first and second sleep doctors she made appointments with echoed the same. It was *normal*. Every new parent had fears. Loads of people had recurring dreams or nightmares.

But there wasn't anything normal about her nightmares. Yes, she may have had the occasional scary dream when she was pregnant. One particularly disturbing nightmare saw Ann sitting by the edge of a bayou with her newborn son in her lap. After counting all his fingers and toes (as new parents do) she lightly kissed the tip of each finger. What would have been a perfectly standard dream became a nightmare as, with each kiss, her child's fingers disconnected from his hand and fell into her lap, bloodless and pale. The dream interpretation websites didn't have an answer to that one. She *knew* what a nightmare was. And what she experienced once her child was born was most definitely *not* a normal nightmare.

It was dark, cold, terrifying, and more real than any dream Ann had ever known.

To avoid the nightmares, Ann would stay up late watching TV. But it never failed. At some point in the night, her eyes would close, and she would drift off to sleep.

***

Something clattered above her, and she eyed the ceiling through the bars of her cage with suspicion. There was a world up there, something moving around in the space she couldn't see, just beyond the top of her cage and the small window. The window was lit brighter than she had ever seen it before, and she wondered if that was a good sign. A soft mewling in the distance awakened an echo of pain in her body and fullness in her soul.

Her baby.

She threw herself at the side of her cage and pushed her face against the hard iron bars, straining to see through the darkness. Unable to see him, she balled her fists and swung at the bars until she collapsed onto her back, exhausted.

They had taken him from her, the strange creatures. Tall, with odd faces, they had ripped her child from her arms, speaking in a language she didn't understand and guffawing with a carelessness that infuriated her. They found humor in her situation. Found pleasure in her terror and agony.

She longed for the times she could hear him cry out because that meant he was still alive and there remained a sliver of hope that she would find him again. She would escape, somehow, and they could return home where there was warmth, safety, and love.

It's not that she was tortured, not physically at least. They hadn't completely left her to die. Every few days they would throw food through the bars, and the bottle of water tied to the side of the cage was almost always full. But it wasn't their home, and she had no idea how she had gotten there or what was going to happen to her and her son.

She stared at the light and waited to hear his voice again.

***

Ann stood over her son's crib and watched him sleep. As he grunted and twitched his lips, she wondered where he was at that moment. Was he also in a cage? Was he hungry and frightened? Her breath caught in her throat, and she reached down to wake him. She couldn't bear the thought of leaving him in that place, though the rational part of her mind told her it wasn't likely at all. People rarely dreamed the same thing as each other. They were all worlds apart, with their own subconscious-created feelings and senses. But still...

Ann changed his diaper and dressed him, cooing over his tiny hands and feet. Big blue eyes stared back at her as he giggled for the first time. Elated, she called Carl into the room.

"What? Is he ok?" Carl asked, breathlessly.

"No, no. Nothing like that. He's perfectly fine."

"Jesus, Ann. You have got to stop waking him up every time you have a nightmare. I get it, the *feelings* are real even if you know the dream isn't. You *feel* like you've lost him. But you didn't. He's right here."

Anne held her son up to her husband as if he were a trophy, ignoring his speech. "It's not that. He *laughed*, Carl."

"Seriously?"

They spent the next hour making silly sounds and singing to their son to see him laugh just one more time. They were happy.

But the fear remained; the thought of falling asleep and dropping into that horrible world.

***

The movement beneath her stilled and the noises above grew in volume and intensity. Things were moving, even if the floor no longer was. She shuffled to the side of the cage and peered between the bars, but it was no use. The rest of the area remained in darkness just like every time before that. Only the edges of cages identical to hers showed on either side. She couldn't even get a good look at her surroundings when they stole her child, even though they carried lights as bright as the sun with them. After she heard the footsteps approaching, she tried to peer through the bars, but the intense light blinded her, leaving sparks and stars whenever she closed her eyes.

She shook away the memory and reached through the cage. Her hand weakly waved in the darkness, reaching out for a child she feared she would never see again.

Whimpering, she dropped back to the cold floor. One leg fell beneath her, but she didn't move to reposition herself even though it was painful to remain there. She didn't think she could move even if she wanted to. Every cell in her body was spent, and she knew the only reason she had lasted as long as she did was the all-consuming desire to find her son. But she was so tired. She shivered as her hands slowly caressed the infant that was no longer there, and she realized the cage was no longer cold. Her thin body no longer ached.

She closed her eyes.

***

Something felt different when Ann awoke the next morning. No longer terrified of her nightmare, a sense of finality and sadness washed over her. She wondered what it all meant as she drove to the daycare, kissed her son goodbye, and headed to work.

She'd just returned from maternity leave a week before and had tons of paperwork to catch up on. Her replacement was less than ideal, a cousin of her boss who couldn't tell his asshole from a hole in the wall. Anne supposed it meant job security for her, but it was going to be a rough few weeks as she tried to undo the messes he had created.

Glancing down at the email on her phone, she grimaced. Boat inspections were her least favorite. But, as her boss had reminded her no less than a dozen times, they worked hard to cover her work while she was out, so the least she could do was cover for Mark while he was out on a "family emergency." Everyone knew there wasn't a damn emergency. Mark was lazy, had too much to drink the night before, and was sleeping off a hangover.

Ann missed drinking. Missed margaritas with her friends and wine with her book club. But while she was still breastfeeding, alcohol was a no-go. At least there was no risk of having a "family emergency" of her own.

The parking lot was mostly empty when she arrived at the docks, and the shipmates were just setting out the platform she would use to board. One of the men rushed toward her carrying a small wooden crate. As he passed, Ann thought she heard something whimpering from within and she froze. When she turned around, the man was already getting into a car that had pulled up to the dock. Gusts from a fierce November wind pushed and pulled on her as she walked to the ship, and she shook her head. Her mind was still playing tricks on her, even when she was awake.

"Hey! Where's Mark?" The captain called out from the deck above her.

"Out sick, you're stuck with me today," Ann replied.

"Well, you're a lot better looking than he is, so I'm not complaining." The captain's eyes shifted down to her chest.

Ann sighed and ducked her head as she stepped onto the deck. Typical boys' club, and there was absolutely no use in pointing out the misogyny. Just get in, do the inspection, and get out.

It was all going smoothly until she entered the cargo hold.

She was in the cage again, terror and hopelessness coursing through her veins.

Ann ran back to the upper deck, leaned over the railing, and dry-heaved over the side of the ship. Thankful she hadn't had any breakfast; she kept her head forward letting the wind whip her hair and wipe away her tears.

"Are you okay?" The captain asked.

Shit. She had forgotten about him.

"Yeah, um. Just a little nausea. I'm good."

Ann took a deep breath and walked back toward the captain.

It was just a nightmare. Nightmares weren't real. But her job and her need to get off that damn ship were very real. The faster she finished her inspection, the faster she could get back to her office.

"See this is why you can't send a woman to do a man's job. Weak constitutions." The captain said, smiling.

Ann pretended not to hear as she rushed past him to the cargo hold.

Every bulb shined as if brand-new, and the scent of bleach permeated the air. Of course, they knew an inspection was coming and had cleaned up. She wasn't sure who had tipped them off, but the whole industry was all about who you knew, so she wasn't surprised at all.

Even better for her, it no longer reminded her of her nightmares. There were cages lined up, but all were clean. It wasn't until she came to the very last row that she saw it tucked away into a corner. The same cage from her nightmare. There was even a water bottle clipped to the side and, above it all, a small round window.

Behind her, the captain cleared his throat. "We 'bout done here? I got shit to do."

Ann turned and studied his face before asking, "What about this one? Why is there a water bottle here? Your log doesn't show a live transport."

Irritation flashed across his face before he forced a laugh, "I don't know. No telling what these dumb-asses get in their heads. But it's clean. You can see that. Nothing out of place, really."

She turned back to the cage and knelt. Fresh bleach still pooled in small spots within, but he was right. Nothing to comment on officially.

When she returned to her office, she was going to call her therapist. It had been a while since they last met and clearly, Ann's mind wasn't set as straight as it used to be.

With an odd sensation that the nightmares were over, Ann went to bed with Carl for the first time in weeks.

***

Euphoric. That was the only way she could describe it. Colors danced around her, and everything looked as if she were seeing it through a plastic bag, all crinkled and hazy. She held her hand up to her face and stared at it, marveling at the design. The incredible wonder of evolution, to leave her with a hand so perfectly functional. She wiggled her fingers and watched the tendons dance beneath her thin skin.

There were no worries, no sadness. Only relaxation and an intense desire to rediscover everything. Like the way her hair grew and the way every cell in her body seemed to live in a Bob Marley song.

She scratched the tip of her nose and imagined a fur blanket wrapped around her as she watched the winter storm rage through her bedroom window.

***

"Sleep well?" Carl asked.

Ann turned away from his morning breath, stood up, and slid into her robe. "Wonderful, actually. I had the best dream."

"Wonderful is good. Wonderful is better than those nightmares."

"It definitely is," Anne smiled as she left the bedroom.

She hadn't thought of that cage in months and knew her therapist had been right. It was a nightmare, it wasn't *real*. Seeing a similar cage on that ship was simply her mind trying to fill in the blanks, trying to make sense of it all. None of it mattered anymore because none of it was real.

They were happy.

***

A sharp pain swam behind her eyes, traveled up her forehead, and spread out into her hair. On the verge of vomiting, she held her stomach and stayed near the bathroom. She'd already missed the mark a few times, judging from the random piles of stench around her. She was exhausted, like when she used to stay at the beach all day and no matter how much water she drank, she still returned sunburned and dehydrated.

Alternating between shivering and sweating, she wasn't sure what was happening to her, only that she wished to all the gods that it would stop. She felt as if she had run three marathons and the act of being alive hurt more than anything she had ever experienced. Bruises bloomed on the insides of both arms, speaking to blown veins beneath. She had hoped to be done with all of that.

She stood and shuffled toward the living room, coming face-to-face with a picture on the end table next to the faded couch. A handsome, happy man holding a small child. She hated that man. Hated who he used to be. Hated who he would never become again.

But she knew that man was gone a long time ago. She mourned him as she dug through the trash on the coffee table for the needle she had prepped earlier, in a moment of weakness.

Moment of weakness.

What a joke.

Her whole life was a fucking moment of weakness. She was delusional if she thought she could win that fight.

Telling herself the little boy in the picture deserved better, she gave up the fight and found a usable vein in her ankle, jabbing the tip of the needle in. She drew the plunger back until blood seeped into the bottom of the needle, then shoved the blood back into her vein along with the heroin.

Soon all feelings of inadequacy and failure were buried in an avalanche of bliss. But unlike previous trips, this one had her flying past the moon. She'd never experienced such intense happiness before. Her new guy had definitely sold her some good shit. As she returned to earth, her breathing slowed, and she was more relaxed than she had ever been. Even in the "before" times. But her aim was off, and the landing didn't stick. Everything went out of focus, and she gagged as she fell to the floor.

The picture of the little boy was the last thing she saw as foam spilled from her lips and everything went black.

***

Ann woke in a sweat and leaped out of bed. She ran to the bathroom and turned on the light, examining her arms and ankles for evidence of what had just happened. But there was nothing. After all, it was just a dream.

The Many Indiscretions of Agent 592

ATTENTION CAFETERIA STAFF:

Please welcome our newest chef, William Scotsman. He has come highly recommended from the Washington site, and we are so excited to have him on our team. Please stop by and say hello if you have a moment.

-MANAGEMENT

————————————————

Mr. Eugene Porter,

I regret to inform you that Operation Pyrosis is not going well. The target has begun the keto diet and is no longer eating in the cafeteria. I cannot administer the poison via spaghetti at this time. I will remain undercover as a cook and await further instruction.

Regretfully,
Agent 592 (William Scotsman)

———————————————

Agent,

Please refrain from emailing confidential information. We discussed this in your last inquiry. I will contact you through the proper channels. Please stand by.

Regards

———————————————

Mr. E.P.,

I've received my reassignment, but people are becoming sus-picious. Apparently, a plumber should know how to use a plunger. Have you used one before? These people are ani-mals. I can't think of one civilized person who would have cause to use such a device. Isn't that what the staff are for? How am I supposed to neutralize Ingrid Vlad as a plumber?

Apologies in advance for the email,

-Agent 592 (W.S.)

————————————————

Agent,

Anyone can use a plunger. A plunger uses basic physics and is not rocket science. Place in the toilet, apply pressure, and pull upward. Hold your position and stop, I repeat: STOP communications via email. This is your final warning.

Regards

____

Mr. E.P.,

Thank you for your instructional email re: proper plunger application. I may now employ the device such that no one will suspect I am an undercover agent.

On a personal note, I am so proud to work for the US Intelligence Agency. I know you said not to tell anyone, but my mother was so excited to hear of what I'm doing for our country. She told her bridge club, but they are upstanding citizens; plus, who would they tell? Our postman, Mike, also knows. He's been our postman for eighteen years. Mother and I are very close with him. Mother bakes him cookies every Christmas and thinks he is very handsome. He is a very trustworthy public servant.

-Agent 592 (W.S.)

Mr. E.P.,

It has been several months since your last communication, and I am losing patience with this plumber bit. Why aren't you responding to my emails?

-Agent 592 (W.S.)

Mr. E.P.,

I think I am being followed. Please provide surveillance assistance. If I could be so bold, I request that Trina Williams from the third floor accompany me. She and I had quite the time at the last Christmas party if you know what I mean. I think she would have danced with me if she hadn't had a family emergency. She's very close to giving me her telephone number, but they keep her busy up there. Every time I've approached her, she has had to make an important phone call. Mother thinks I should find a nice redhead. I quite agree.

-Agent 592 (W.S.)

––––––––––

Mr. E.P.,

As I have still not heard back, I will assume you are going to send Trina Williams. Can you get me the phone number of HR? I can't remember the policies regarding inter-office romance.

-Agent 592 (W.S.)

––––––––––

Mr. E.P.,

I'm starting to worry. I tried calling you, but I think I have the wrong number. Also, my access code has stopped working for the online portal. Can you please look into this? In the meantime, Operation Pyrosis is still at a standstill. We had quite the backup in the restrooms after Taco Tuesday. We started out with thirty gallons of refried beans and ended with half a pint if that gives you any idea of the aftermath. On a related note, I would like to formally express my displeasure regarding this cover. I have never in my life felt such disgust, not even when Agent Michael and I were knee-deep in the sewers during Operation Quiver.

Ingrid is still on keto and has foregone the tacos. I've been unable to keep an eye on her, but I will not give up. You can count on me.

Please tell Trina I am still waiting for her.

-Agent 592 (W.S.)

———————————

ATTENTION CAFETERIA STAFF:

Please welcome our newest chef, Michael Lindly. He has come highly recommended from the St. Louis site, and we are so excited to have him on our team. Please stop by and say hello if you have a moment. I hear his Spaghetti Bolognese is to die for.

-MANAGEMENT

————————————

Mr. E.P.,

I see that you have sent Michael Lindly instead of Trina. I thought we had an understanding.

When will I be able to return to the kitchen? If I have yet to make it clear, I do not enjoy pretending to be a plumber.

Ingrid came into the cafeteria yesterday and I do not like the way Michael was looking at her. He's here to assist, not take over my operation. Please remind him of this.

-Agent 592 (W.S.)

———————————

E,

The spaghetti has been delivered. A second batch will soon be served.

Thank you,

M.

———————————

Autopsy of William Andrew Scotsman

Conclusion: After a review of the autopsy findings and available investigative

information, it is the opinion of this
coroner that William Albert Scotsman
(42-year-old white male) died as a
result of complications associated with
cyanide toxicity. It is unclear how the
decedent ingested such large doses of
cyanide.

Manner of death: internal asphyxia as
a result of cyanide toxicity.

Octosquatch

Jennifer Martin and Yolanda Jiminez didn't realize it yet, but their decision to leave the trail that hot day in August would cost them both their lives.

"Come on, slowpoke," laughed Jennifer as she tugged on Yolanda's hand.

They ducked beneath branches and side-stepped large rocks in their way. The canopy of trees stretched above them, filtering the harsh sun into a soft light that enveloped them, leaving deep shadows just out of reach. They couldn't see it, but the East Cascade Mountain Range loomed in the distance, much closer than either of them realized.

"Almost there," Jennifer said.

"How do you know about this place again?"

"I told you, Brad and Eileen come out here all the time. They said it's the perfect-"

The women emerged from the forest, stepping into a small clearing wide enough for the sun to reach down and kiss their upturned faces. Soft green moss carpeted the ground beneath their feet and birds tweeted to each other from the trees. All around them, almost in a perfect circle, stood the tall fir trees and beyond that, endless miles of the Blue Ridge Forest.

"This is gorgeous," whispered Yolanda.

Jennifer nodded in agreement, her eyes wide as she took in the beauty around them. Still holding tightly to Yolanda's hand, she pulled her closer. The two women looked into each other's eyes, close enough to feel their hot breath on each other's faces.

"*This* is gorgeous," said Jennifer as she closed the gap between them and kissed her. Jennifer's hands eagerly sought out the other woman's curves. They fell softly onto the moss-padded ground and melted into each other's embrace. Yolanda pulled Jennifer's shirt off and tossed it behind her then paused, staring into the trees beyond.

"Don't stop!" protested Jennifer, "What are you doing?" Her back arched as she fumbled with the zipper on her jeans.

"Shh! Did you hear that?" whispered Yolanda, her brow furrowed.

"It's the *forest*, Yolanda. It makes noises, now-"

A twig snapped nearby and a faint smacking sound followed, like someone chewing gum in that annoying way, with their mouth wide open.

"I'm gonna check it out, wait here," said Yolanda as she grabbed Jennifer's shirt and tossed it to her.

Yolanda crept towards the edge of the clearing. Jennifer pulled her shirt back over her head, taking her eyes off her girlfriend for a moment, but when the shirt's collar cleared her eyes, there was no sign of Yolanda. Another branch snapped and the wet, suckling noise sounded closer than before. Jennifer had taken one step toward the tree line when she heard a scream.

Jennifer, frozen with fear and confusion, stared at the tree line. When her mind caught up with what her ears had taken in, she ran towards the sound.

She was almost at the edge of the clearing when more twigs and leaves rustled. Jennifer paused and squinted through the thick brush, hoping to see Yolanda. Hoping she was okay and just messing around.

"Yo, come on. Stop screwing with me," Jennifer's voice shook. "Yol<u>an</u>-"

But it wasn't her friend that was coming toward her. Something else emerged from the tree line and stepped into the clearing just a few feet from Jennifer. There, towering above her, was a hideous creature. Eight long, grey tentacles reached out to her with that sick, wet, smacking sound. Each one covered with contracting circles. Her eyes followed the tentacles to their ends, but they curved behind a solid back, covered in dark matted fur dripping with water. Running down from there were two thick legs, equally covered in fur though not as wet. And at their end, two hairy feet. Above the tentacles were broad shoulders, arms covered in hair, and a face... a face like something out of a nightmare. Piercing gray eyes, almost white, stood out from the dark brown fur on its face. The thing's chest rose and fell with each huffing sound from its gaping mouth.

Jennifer turned to run, but the tentacles were faster. Two grabbed her arms and suctioned to her skin. Another reached around her neck and pulled her backward, straight into the open arms of the hairy beast. All went dark as it tore into the soft flesh of her neck and pulled away, blood and gristle stretching between its sharp teeth and the gaping wound.

The creature feasted as the sun's long golden rays flashed and then disappeared behind the mountains in the distance.

***

"Everyone, just calm down!" roared Maria Perez, Mayor of the small town of New Bedford, Washington.

"No one has ever calmed down by being told to calm down," mumbled Denny Hawkins. He and his wife, Wilma, sat in the front row of the school's auditorium.

She leaned towards him, "*Calm down*, Denny." and winked.

Denny smirked at his wife and, as she returned her gaze to the Mayor, glanced back to see his girlfriend, Paula Lowell, fuming behind her sunglasses from her seat three rows behind them. He shrugged and turned around. She would get over it, it's not like he could ignore his wife. They were in public, after all, and with Reverend Fuller sitting right next to him.

"Now, let's do this in an orderly manner," Boomed Maria from a too-close microphone in her hand. "You wanna talk, stand up and wait to be called on."

Seven citizens jumped from their seats, all glaring at her.

"All right, you in the blue shirt... let's have it."

"Name's Linda. Nineteen of my horses were killed! NINETEEN! Is anyone gonna actually take care of this thing or are me and my boys gonna have to do it ourselves?"

"Look, we've called down the crew from Seattle. They're the best bear-hunters around here and they'll do a much more efficient job of this. The last thing we need is a damn militia group botching it up and getting in their way," answered Maria.

Linda plopped down in a huff, then leaned toward the man sitting next to her and whispered something in his ear.

Maria turned to a bald man standing quietly in the back row, "Ok, you, there in the back."

"Yeah, I want to ask what's being done about the earthquake damage. The bridge is a mess, how are people supposed to come into my store when they can't even cross the bridge?"

"We're working on the street repairs as fast as we can, but you know these things take time," answered Maria.

"But what about my store?" yelled the man.

"Let's take this offline, we'll talk after the town hall is over, okay? I'll see what we can do to prioritize that street."

The man mumbled something beneath his breath and sat back down.

Maria scanned the other five people still standing. "OK you, uhh... " She squinted and leaned forward over the podium, "Henry, right?"

"Yeah, look, I don't give a shit about horses," he gestured towards the woman who had just spoken, "or cattle, or missing dogs," he waved his arm around him to encompass everyone packed into the auditorium. "I mean, don't get me wrong... I'm sorry and all, but what's done is done. Nothin' is bringin' 'em back, you know? What I need to know, is if the Fair is still happening."

Maria stepped back from the podium and handed the microphone to a man standing beside her.

"I'm Bill Lincoln, City Secretary. Yes, we *are* still going forward with the State Fair. We have complete faith in the team from Seattle to take care of this... *problem* before Saturday. There have been no indications that the bear has hunted in this direction, all of the attacks have happened miles outside of town."

An elderly man stood up, leaned on the back of the chair in front of him for support, and interrupted Bill, "Now how the hell can you say you know where it's gonna go? You can't know that, just like you can't promise they'll catch 'im. We need to cancel the Fair, or that blood is gonna be on *your* hands!" He covered his mouth as a dry cough heaved from his lungs.

A few people shouted their agreement with the old man, while the majority of the crowd shouted to keep the Fair going. Maria stepped back to the podium and banged her hand on the microphone before the shouting died down, leaving the townspeople still grumbling low whispers to each other.

"Look, as of right now, the State Fair is still on. The only thing we're doing differently is to open up the field behind Sawyer's for cars since the parking lot won't be fixed in time. The earthquake is bad timing, and these bear attacks are unfortunate. But I assure you, we are safe and we *are* going to have the State Fair. We need this revenue to carry us through the winter, and all of you know that."

The auditorium once again erupted into chaos, the noise overpowering any single person's voice. As Maria continued to bang on the microphone, the back doors burst open and a woman ran through the crowd and toward the stage.

"Maria! You have to help me. I tried going down to the Police Department, but they said I can't file nothing for two days, but I just *know* something's happened to Jennifer!"

Maria stopped banging on the microphone and leaned down, giving up on any semblance of a productive town hall. She covered the top of the mic with her hand. "Isobel? What's going on?"

"Jennifer!" Isobel wailed, "She stayed the night at Yolanda's house but was supposed to come home this morning and she won't answer her pho ne... and I can't find Yolanda's mom! What if... the bear..."

"Hey, now they're probably fine. I'm sure they didn't go into the woods." Maria stood up and scanned the thinning crowd before leaning towards the microphone, "Katherine! Katherine Jiminez! Yes, you. Can you come up here please?"

Katherine elbowed her way through the people starting to leave like a salmon swimming upstream. Her eyes widened when she recognized Isobel Martin.

"Isobel? What's wrong?"

"Katherine, have you or Yolanda heard from Jennifer today?" Maria asked.

Katherine looked from Isobel to Maria, and back again. "But... the girls are with *you*, right? Right?"

"Oh god... oh god-" Isobel wailed. "No. I thought they were with you!" She turned to Maria, "You have to do something!

"Okay, okay, let's see..." Maria pulled her phone from her pocket, fingers flying across the screen as she scrolled through her contact list.

Katherine also pulled her phone out and dialed her husband. He answered on the first ring. "Joe, have you heard from Yolanda?" She listened, then looked at Isobel and shook her head.

Maria slipped her phone back into her pocket. "Ok, let's go to the Police Station, Chief Rutherford said to come on down and ask for him."

***

"Ok, has everyone signed in and gone over the procedures?" Police Chief Larry Rutherford addressed the crowd of forty-two people in front of him at the edge of the Blue Ridge Forest. "Now, get with your assigned partners and head out."

The search party had been assembled within thirty minutes after a missing person's report was filed. Friends and family of Jennifer Martin and Yolanda Jiminez, as well as half the New Bedford Police Department, had shown up.

Larry turned towards the officer standing to his left. "Jackson, you and I will check the clearing. Some friends of Jennifer's came up and said they might be there. It's a small chance, but we gotta check it. We'll get there a lot faster with Albert," he gestured towards a large man standing next to an ATV with two rifles affixed to the roof.

As they were walking toward the ATV, another officer ran up to them and shoved a radio in Larry's hand, "Chief, you're gonna want to hear this."

The Chief pressed the button on the side of the radio, "This is Chief Rutherford, go ahead."

"Yeah, Chief. You can call off the search party," A voice crackled through the radio. "We've got some hikers that just called in a... scene. It sounds like the girls you're looking for."

"Shit," muttered Larry. "Okay, what's the location?"

"The clearing, over by the Saginaw River."

Larry hung his head as he handed the radio back to the officer.

"Chief? Do we need to call everyone back?"

"No, let's check this out first. Albert, let's go."

The men were silent as the ATV flew down the trails and Larry studied the forest around them. When they were close to the clearing, he tapped on Albert's shoulder to stop.

"This is where we walk," Larry said as he and Albert collected the rifles from the top of the vehicle.

"Are you sure?" Jackson asked, glancing around at the forest surrounding them before following the others away from the trail.

"Yeah, I'm sure. What, you think only kids nowadays know about this spot? This was *the* place back in my day."

"But... what about the bear? Maybe we shouldn't be out here," whispered Jackson as he continued to scan the trees.

"Jackson, chill out. The attacks have been over on the East side, that's miles away from-"

Emerging from the tree line, the men were greeted with a grisly sight. Shredded red and dark blue cloth was strewn around the clearing, and a human vertebrae lay on top of a pile of blood-covered bits of skin, bone, and hair.

"Jesus Christ is that-" whispered Albert, before vomiting at his feet.

Larry took a deep breath, "I think so. Jackson, do you have the notes on the girls' clothing?"

"Jackson?"

Jackson was staring at the still-perfectly braided strand of hair lying on the side of the pool of blood. At one end, a small hair tie, and at the other... what could have only been a square of scalp, held it all together.

"Jackson!"

His head snapped away from the braid and he looked at Larry. "Yeah..." Jackson pulled the notepad from the pocket on the front of his uniform and flipped it open. "Jennifer Martin was wearing a red shirt and blue jeans. Yolanda Jiminez was wearing a white shirt and blue jean shorts." He looked up from the notes and stared again at the pile of flesh and bone on the grass in front of him, all that remained of Jennifer Martin.

"Shit," whispered Jackson.

"Shit is right," said Larry.

The men investigated the clearing, but it wasn't until they searched the surrounding area that they came upon another stack of bones and bloody gristle. This time, it was only a single piece of white cloth hanging from a branch that they could identify as being a part of Yolanda Jiminez. The rest was red with blood, even the scalp lying on top of the vertebrae. Placed there almost purposefully, like some sort of trophy.

***

As the sun set over the mountains, darkness filtered down onto the field where the State Fair was to be held. Carnival rides sat empty, the towering Ferris Wheel and Tilt-A-Whirl waited silently for eager riders with fists full of tickets. Sno-cone and hot dog stands were boarded up, the flags affixed to them flapping in the wind. Most of the carnies were under the Big Top on the North side of the lot, drinking and dancing. Others were already in bed, exhausted from a day spent setting up the booths, tents, and rides.

At the edge of the field, where the low-cut grass met the wild tree line, something stirred in the brush. The creature crept forward, weak and hungry. Eight tentacles rustled the grass behind its body, dry and cracked. It crawled toward the southern end of the property, where a faint smell of water lingered. There it found a tank of water, at least five feet deep, and full of small fish. Short poles leaned against it and a sign advertised "Five minutes of fishing for only 2 tickets." The creature climbed over the side of the tank and dropped into the water with a large splash. As it sank below the surface, the last of the dry tentacles cleared the side of the tank and eased into the water behind it.

A light came on in a small camper parked nearby and the door cracked open. A bearded woman's head peeked out into the night, shouting "Who's there? Jason? I told you to leave me alone!" When the night around her remained silent, she slammed the door, turned the light back off, and returned to her cot.

In the tank, water fanned out in ripples, splashing against the sides before easing back to the center, repeating until they slowly flattened out into a smooth, mirror-like surface.

***

"See, I told you everything would work out," Maria boasted.

"Look, no offense, but I don't think we can say we're in the clear here," Larry said.

Maria grinned at the family walking past them, letting them get out of earshot before seething, "Would you keep your voice down? Everything is fine. You can't prove those girls were killed by the bear. For all we know, it's still over on the East end."

"I'm telling you, this isn't a bear we're dealing with! Bears don't act like-"

"What about rabies? Maybe it's a rabid bear."

"Can you fucking *hear* yourself? Look, just don't come crying to me when the shit hits the fan." Larry walked away without giving Maria a chance to respond.

"Everything's all right people, go on in and have fun!" Maria beamed at a young couple who had stopped after hearing Larry's outburst.

Past the ticket booth, there was no evidence that anyone was thinking about the two young women who had been mauled to death, or the possibility of a bear, rabid or not. Most of the people there had never even heard of Jennifer Martin or Yolanda Jiminez, much less cared about their deaths. All they knew was that they had brought their family to eat fried foods, spend a little money, and have a good time. Spilled popcorn littered the ground near one of the snack kiosks and the sugary scent of cotton candy weaved around everyone as they threw darts at balloons pinned to a board, waited in line for a ride, or bought tickets to one of the shows.

The "Fishing Frenzy" tank at the far end of the Fair was one of the most popular activities with the kids, especially the younger ones. Two tickets could buy five minutes of fishing, which sounded a little silly considering all the rivers and lakes around them that the kids could fish in for as long as they wanted to, for zero tickets. But there they stood, a line of twenty youngsters waiting their turn at the poles. Only a few of them could fish at a time, what with the possibility of tangled lines and all.

A baby squealed as his mother held him up over the edge of the tank and dipped his toes in the cool water while one of the workers peered at the bottom of the tank, confused.

"Hey, Gabe! Come here and take a look at somethin', would ya?"

"What is it?" his coworker asked as he headed over.

"How many fish did you put in here yesterday?"

"I don't know, man. All of 'em I guess."

"You guess?"

"Ok, ok... me and Roberta fried a couple up. But they was small, what's it matter just two little fish?"

"Gabe, there's more than *two* missing. Look." He pointed to the bottom of the tank, void of anything but silt and a few leaves.

The other man leaned over the edge and whistled low, "Shiiit. Ok, just don't say nothin' to the kids. We can act like they're not bitin' good today. We'll figure it out later, you see this line we got waitin' on us right now?"

With that, they both moved to help the next group of kids with their fishing poles, neither noticing the soaked ground behind the tank or the enormous, wet footprints that trailed off behind the row of tents.

***

"I'm just saying, it looked like you two were having a good 'ole time." Paula pouted, "When are you going to leave her, Denny?"

"Did you not see Reverend Fuller sitting right there? What am I supposed to do… ignore her?" Denny replied, pulling Paula into his embrace.

She feigned offense, letting her hands hang to her sides while he wrapped his arms around her and nuzzled her neck. "I'm just saying, I'm not gonna wait around forever, you know."

"Look we didn't come back here to talk, did we? Now come here…"

Neither Denny nor Paula noticed the creature lurking in the shadows behind them until wet tentacles wrapped around both of their necks and squeezed. The harsh crack of bones drowned out their final whimpers, and their bodies slumped to the ground before they realized what was happening. Still satiated from the fish eaten earlier, the creature left them in the dirt and slipped through an opening in a nearby tent.

Lit only by a few battery-operated lights fashioned to look like flickering candles, the interior of the black tent was dark and bustling with people. They made their way to the exhibits, single-file, pausing at each stage, table, or jar in front of them. A barker could be heard outside the front of the tent shouting, "Freak Show! Come see the bearded lady and the two-headed chicken! Feast your eyes on the world's fattest man and the world's smallest woman! Be among the first to peer at the malformed body of the Egyptian baby who caused its own mother to die of fright after casting her eyes upon it!" His voice droned on as the crowd shuffled forward.

The creature stood in the corner, studying the people in front of him. A young man noticed him there and dragged his girlfriend over to look.

"Look, Rachel! What do you think this thing is?"

"I don't know, there's no sign or nothin'."

"This is lame, you know all this shit is fake, right? Let's get out of here."

They turned to go, and the creature slipped back through the opening in the tent and back out into the night air.

***

Maria stood in line for the Ferris wheel beside her husband, Anthony. Her eyes darted around the crowds, stopping at Henry Miller. He was staring at her, his brow furrowed and tense.

"Maybe he was right," whispered Maria.

"What?" Anthony asked.

"Maybe he was right. If something happens and we knew there was a chance and could have warned all of these people…"

"Maria, look at me." He pulled her toward him and lifted her chin. "Everything is fine. You know Henry Miller's got a few screws loose. That man wouldn't trust the Pope."

"Maybe…"

"Look, you've worked your ass off, and you deserve a little break too, right? Doesn't the Mayor get to have a little fun also?"

"Yeah, you're right. I'm sure it's fine." They moved to the front of the line, handed their tickets to the operator, and climbed into the hanging chair.

Maria clutched the safety bar in front of her a little more tightly than she needed to, as the towering wheel turned to allow another couple to load and the chair swayed in the wind.

Below them, Wilma Hawkins flagged down Officer Jackson.

"Have you seen Denny? I can't find him anywhere." She asked.

"No ma'am, but I'll keep my eye out for him," Jackson replied.

"He's probably with that whore Paula. Oh, don't look so shocked. Of course, I know. The whole friggin' town knows. If you find him, you just tell him I went on home without 'im." Wilma turned on her heels and headed towards the exit.

Jackson was watching her storm off and shaking his head when the first scream pierced the night air. The creature had emerged from behind the tents and was standing just below the Ferris Wheel. One scream turned into thousands as everyone watched the sasquatch with tentacles reach out and rip a chunk of skin and bone from the neck of the Ferris Wheel operator.

Larry, observing from a caramel apple booth about thirty feet away, jumped over the wooden railing and ducked behind the counter, pressing the call button on his radio.

"Yeah, dispatch? I need everyone out to the Fair NOW, locked and loaded. And call Linda Massey, and see if she still knows those bear hunters she talked about at the meeting. We need a bigger gun than my little pistol here. Got it? Ok, I gotta go. Call Linda!"

He peeked over the edge of the booth in time to see the creature pull a man from his seat on the Ferris Wheel. It was still turning, bringing everyone closer to the ground, some lucky enough to roll back around on the upswing and miss the tentacles and teeth. Others weren't as lucky.

Maria watched in horror as the creature pulled a man from the chair directly in front of her and her husband. As they passed by, the tentacles brushed her shoulders but the animal was too busy with his teeth buried in the poor man's neck to notice. Maria and Anthony held their breath as the ride creaked, swinging them past the thing and back toward the sky once again.

The air, previously filled with laughter and organ music, devolved quickly into screams and gunshots. Larry and Jackson fired their handguns as they ran toward the creature. Stopping to plant his feet and square his arms, Larry fired again. It bellowed with pain, but dropped the dead man and ran towards Jackson, who hadn't stopped beside Larry. Grey tentacles flew behind him and giant feet plowed into the ground with every step, his nostrils flaring with anger and his eyes rimmed with red. Two small holes, one in his shoulder and another in his chest, dripped blood into his thick fur.

"Jackson! Pull back!" Larry shouted.

Too late, Jackson turned to run away from the creature, but the long tentacles closed the distance between them faster than he could run and jerked him backward. Claws reached out from behind Jackson, dug into his cheeks, and pulled up. He was dead before he hit the ground, his cheekbones jutted out from his tattered skin and bloody holes filled the space where his eyes had been.

Larry fired again, emptying his clip into the animal as it closed the distance between them. The animal's huffing, hot breath was inches away from Larry's face, the tentacles encircling his body, and claws scraping his skin from outstretched arms when another shot rang out. The animal staggered back, and the tentacles dropped from Larry's skin. Albert stepped out from behind the snow-cone stand, the tip of his shotgun still smoking.

Still strapped into their seats, Maria and Anthony struggled to free themselves from the safety bar, barely slipping out in time to jump to the ground as the swinging chair turned again toward the sky. For once, she was grateful Albert went around town with those damn guns strapped to his ATV.

Albert cocked his shotgun and took aim. Larry, bleeding but reloaded and ready, joined him. A flurry of bullets flew through the air as the creature's body swayed back and forth, trying to stay on its feet. From deep inside, he managed one last, painful roar before falling to the ground.

Maria ran to Larry's side, "Are you ok?"

"Fucking OctoSquatch attacked me, no I'm not ok."

Shrill sirens rang out in the distance, growing louder.

"The ambulance will be here soon, leave me alone," Larry said.

"Look, I don't know why you're mad at me. This isn't my fault." Maria put her hands on her hips.

"Guys..." Anthony whispered.

"It's not your fault? It *is* your damn fault! I told you we weren't safe." Larry said.

"Guys!" Anthony screamed.

"What?" Larry and Maria turned in unison.

Anthony pointed to the animal. No longer on the ground, it was limping toward them with fire in its eyes. The tentacles struggled to lift themselves to attack position.

By the time Albert raised his shotgun again, booming shots rang out from behind him. Linda and her friends had arrived, with guns powerful enough to take down a bear... or an Octosquatch.

The creature fell again, its face a mash of blood and fur, any features obliterated. The back of its head was blown open, and bone fragments and grey chunks fell onto the ground behind it. The eight tentacles twitched in the dust.

They moved closer to the dead creature, in awe of the size and nature of the thing.

"How did you get here so fast?" Larry asked.

"I told you, we knew this shit was gonna go down, just didn't know where...and damn sure didn't know it was gonna be *this* freak of nature," Linda nudged a dry tentacle with the edge of her boot. "We were loaded up and about to head out to the forest when your dispatcher called us. What the fuck is this thing, anyway?"

"I don't know, but looks like we have company," Maria answered, pointing to the small crowd that had gathered. Almost every one of them had their cell phones out, flashes strobing as they took pictures of the creature. "This'll be all over the place by morning."

"You think so? Think anyone will really believe it?" Anthony asked.

Maria's eyes twinkled as she looked at Larry. "Maybe they shouldn't...."

"What are you talking about? It's here, right in front of us." Larry answered.

"But, what if the body...*disappears*. Think about it. Who wants to come to a town where there might be more of these...*things* somewhere? No one. But what if we let out that it was a hoax? Think of the crowds we'll have next year! Think of the publicity!"

"People *died*! You really need help, you know that? I'm going home," Larry grumbled as he walked away.

Maria ran after him, "No, but listen, this could be *great* for the town!"

Three Acts

The town streaks by in a blur of color as the train flies down the tracks, resembling more a Rothko painting and less my entire life's history. I was born in the sparse beige building up ahead on the left. That's what they told me, anyway. I was too young to know, of course. I purchased the crumpled ticket in my hand at almost the exact same spot where my mother left me when I was only two days old. She packed me into a small cardboard box and dropped me at the train station like a package out for delivery, swaddled with newspapers to protect me from the late fall chill. Scrawled in her childish handwriting on the side was a note:

"Please take her."

That was it. Just three words. That's all I have of my mother, a tattered note tucked inside a plastic bag and zipped into a side pocket of my purse. I have carried her with me always. This is all I know of who I am. Who I should be.

I'm not blaming the Hendersons or implying they didn't love me. They did, in the only way they knew how. Father a little too much, on the days Mother was at bridge and he opened a few too many bottles. In the mornings, she would mend my torn clothing and change the bedsheets so the smears of blood wouldn't stare at her, accusatory.

There were brothers and sisters throughout the years. None worse or better than the rest, or more or less memorable than the next. It all just happened, my life. I have had no more control over it than I do this train.

It goes, I go.

It stops, I stop.

It doesn't care how I feel, or what I want to do, or who I want to love. Or if I even know how. I'm encased in a block of ice, frozen against hurt and disappointment. Whatever happens, I stay the same. Hard, cold, and tired.

So tired.

On the other side of the window, grass blurs into green blobs and the clouds rush to catch up in a swirl of blue and white. This train is my second direct act in taking control. *My* decision, *my* choice, instead of reacting to everything and everyone that ever wanted a piece of me. I couldn't die in that town that had already claimed so much of who I was, and who I should have been.

And I no longer want to live.

I check the zippered pocket of my purse and caress the hard steel grip of the handgun I stole from Father this morning before I left their home after I shot them. That was my first act of taking things back.

This will be the tool of my salvation.

The new town, wherever I end up, will be absent of anyone who has ever abandoned me or claimed pieces they did not deserve.

I will end things with my own hand and on my own terms. Knowing what lies ahead, I smile. My life. My hand. My way.

I choose this.

The Dinner Rush

Victoria slammed the heavy door behind her as she stomped into the narrow alley behind Luigi's. With fingers trembling in the frigid night air, it took her two tries before she was able to light her cigarette. She jerked her coat zipper up to her neck and huddled against the closed door, sucking on the cigarette as if it were her own personal heater. As she exhaled, her breath steamed into the cold air, braided itself into the discarded smoke, and danced off into the night.

"Oof!" she stumbled backward as the door behind her opened with a jolt and a rush of warmth.

"Look, you don't have to fall into my arms. I told you I'm ready when you are for that date." Alonzo winked at her, keeping his strong hands on her waist long after she had righted herself.

Damn, he smelled nice. Like pine trees, and chocolate, and...

She took a step back, mumbling, "That shit doesn't work on me". She searched his deep brown, flecked with gold on the edges, eyes. *God, he was gorgeous.* She looked down at the cigarette between her fingers and cleared her throat. "Go try that smooth shit out on one of your other girls."

Alonzo held his hands up in mock defeat, "Well if you won't go out with me, can you at least gimme a light?" He extracted a pack of cigarettes from the black apron around his narrow waist and tapped them on his palm.

"So, did you hear what happened in Florida?" he asked as the lighter clicked shut with a flick of his wrist.

"The Mars shuttle? Yeah, they said everyone was dead."

"I heard they were blue." He took a drag off his cigarette. When he returned her lighter, his fingers brushed against hers, sending lightning bolts up her arm.

"Blue? Like... a smurf?"

"Yeah, but just their faces."

"Weird, do-"

The door to the restaurant jerked open and a thin woman poked her head out, "Guys, are you coming back to work anytime this year? You only get five minutes for a break, you know."

"Calm your tits, Amanda, we're coming," Alonzo winked at Victoria before following the hostess back into the restaurant. She rubbed her cigarette out on the brick wall and shoved the remaining half back into the pack before going in.

Halfway through the dinner rush, when Victoria had just come through the kitchen doors with a tray full of Chianti-braised short ribs and potato gnocchi, a blood-curdling scream came from the patio. Patrons froze with their forks and glasses halfway to their mouths. The bartender halted in the middle of pouring a double of scotch, the amber drops unnoticed as they splashed out of the small glass and onto the bar below. Amanda stood in front of the seating chart with the dry-erase marker poised in midair, threatening to dry out and render itself useless.

A young man burst through the front doors, his long leather jacket flapping behind him in the wind like a cape, before collapsing in front of the hostess stand and breaking the spell. Alonzo looked over his own food-laden tray and made eye contact with Victoria.

Before the young man fell to the floor, everyone in the restaurant had seen his face.

Covered in sores, some seeping pus through jagged broken skin, others on the verge of bursting, the guy's face was a bright blue landmine.

A little boy, not a day over four years old, was standing just inside the front door next to a man and a woman waiting for their seat, his hands holding each of theirs. He stared up at them through wayward strands of orange-red hair, eyes wide while they both clawed at their faces.

The chaos around them intensified. Pedestrians from outside were running into the restaurant, while patrons and servers were running out. Most had no idea where they were going or what they were running from. An elderly woman clawing at her cheeks bumped into Victoria, causing her to drop her tray onto the table behind her, narrowly missing the middle-aged couple who had sprung up from their seats. Alonzo ran towards her, gripped her elbow, and pulled her towards the rear of the restaurant where the door to the wine cellar stood open like a beacon in the fog.

As the heavy wooden door slammed shut, it was as if someone had taken a dimmer switch to the insanity only a few feet away. Muffled screams whispered through the door into the cellar, and they could no longer hear chairs and tables falling over as bodies and furniture crashed together. Once Victoria's eyes adjusted to the dim interior, she saw waiters, cooks, the bussers, and a couple of strange faces that she assumed were diners huddled together. All eyes were on the large door, vibrating from a steady pounding of fists on the other side.

Leon leaned against a large cabinet and pushed, not noticing as his chef's hat fell to the floor. James, the bartender, leaned against it with him and together they managed to slide the heavy cabinet in front of the door. Two wine bottles rolled off the top shelf and crashed to the floor, throwing shards of glass and liquid across the ceramic tile. Reds. Heavy scents of caramel, black currant, and wafts of something earthy permeated the air.

The small crowd in the wine cellar moved towards the far wall. As far away as they could get from the screams on the other side, the broken glass on the floor, and the sticky sweet aromas filling the small space. They huddled against the wall of bottles, speaking only in whispers, not wanting to reveal their hiding place to whatever terrors lurked on the other side.

"What *is* that?"

"You think it's like Florida?"

"They said everyone was *dead* when the shuttle came back."

Victoria remained silent, barely noticing the warmth from Alonzo's hand as he held hers tightly.

Alonzo jerked his free hand towards the back of the room, gesturing for everyone to shut up, as he leaned against the hard door. The edges of the cabinet dug into his hip while he strained to press his ear against the smooth wooden surface.

Silence filled the space as echoes of screams faded off into the distance. Alonzo braced himself, released Victoria's hand, and pushed against the cabinet blocking the door.

"No! Don't open it!" An older woman with short white hair, perfectly coifed, screamed at him. Drawn butter dripped from her chin onto a lobster bib still tied around her neck. A small red-headed little boy stood next to her; his eyes wide with wonder.

"I'm just going to peek, see what's going on." Alonzo paused, staring into Victoria's eyes. She nodded. With a groan, he moved the cabinet a few inches to the side. "See, I can't even open the door all the way. We're fine. Just a few more inches".

He leaned into the small gap as the crowd held their breath behind him. The back of his head cocked to one side, then the other before he pulled himself back into the room.

"Nothing. There's no one out there." When Alonzo turned around, all eyes were on him, and the bib-adorned woman was crying.

"What? What's wrong?"

Victoria reached towards him before pulling her hands together against her chest and taking a step back. "Zo, your face..."

"What? What's wrong with my face?"

Bright blue patches had spread across his forehead and were inching down his nose.

The blue skin festered and sizzled as it spread across his cheeks.

"Get it off!" He cried, scraping at his face with his fingernails, but the rash ate its way across his skin, devouring everything in its path. Angry pink flesh shone through the blue ooze and dark blood. That, too, dissolved, leaving a bright white cheekbone to poke through into the soft light of the wine cellar. With a final, gut-wrenching wail, he collapsed on the floor at Victoria's feet as the blue fizzled out, its job now complete.

She dropped to her feet and put a hand on his chest. *It wasn't possible, he couldn't be...gone. He was just holding her hand not five minutes before.*

Victoria rubbed the back of her hand against her face, smearing the tears across her cheek. She stood back up and turned around to face the small crowd. They were all staring, at her, their eyes wide with fear.

"What?"

She could feel a white-hot pain inching across her forehead. As one, the crowd pressed against each other, unable to get away from Victoria, and what was left of Alonzo.

All but a small red-headed little boy, who stood away from the others, eyes twinkling with mischief, and a grin slowly spreading across his cherubic face.

When the Swell Breaks

This wasn't how I planned to spend my thirty-ninth birthday, but here I am. I've lived a good life, I think. I never finished getting my degree, but I have a job I love.

Loved.

My home isn't a mansion, but it's comfortable and enough. Two children, one of each, boy and girl. Check and check. Loving husband, check.

He's standing in the hospital corridor now, talking with two of the doctors while I'm supposed to be sleeping. His eyes swing towards the room, and through the hatched lines on the window, I can see his face. The last few months have aged him, taken him to that place from which you can never return. He isn't surprised I'm awake. We both know it's time. We've known for a few weeks now, that this is the best option, and I've already said goodbye to the kids.

At first, I was selfish, and heartbroken that they might not remember me. They're only two and three years old. But after I had more time to think about it, I hope they *didn't* remember me. Not like this. This sterile hospital room with beeping machines and harsh lights, drowning everyone who enters in its sea of hopelessness. Away from all of this, years from now, they'll be ok.

But William, sweet William. He'll remember every bit of it, I know him like the back of my hand. He was such a joyful man, and I've taken that from him. Me, and this damn tumor that they said would keep growing, taking over my brain like a parasite until I wouldn't know who I was anymore. Machines could keep me alive for a little while, but I don't want that for William, or for the kids. They need to be able to move on, and one day they will.

Not today.

William comes into the room with a doctor close behind him.

"What's it going to be then, eh?" I try to smile but the weight of it all pushes the edges of my lips downward. My voice shakes. "Miracle cure or sleeping potion?" I know there is no cure.

William lowers the bed rail and climbs in, squeezing me in his embrace until it's hard to breathe. We stare at each other and the swell breaks, pushing tears down both of our faces. He places his hands on my pale cheeks and kisses me softly. I don't want to go. I want to stay here with him forever.

I turn to the doctor and nod.

Step by Step

Maeve scowled at her cell phone in disgust before shoving it back into her purse.

You'd think a building as nice as hers could afford a few signal boosters, but every fucking time she stepped into one of their elevators, her phone cut off. She usually took the stairs to avoid the awkward social interactions of being stuck in a box with people she barely knew, but her feet hurt that day. Maeve wore her new red heels to work without breaking them in first and had instantly regretted her choice.

She made a mental note to call her mother back as soon as she got to her floor and, for the first time, glanced around at the other passengers she would be forced to interact with.

Maeve smiled. Maybe the elevator ride wouldn't be so bad after all. To her right stood Paul Morgan. He lived down the hall from her, so she ran into him every now and then at the swimming pool, the mailroom, or the gym downstairs. Paul was quite possibly the hottest man in the building, and single ever since his wife had died in a car accident the year before. Maeve figured she'd give it another month or so before making a move on him, out of respect for the deceased.

He looked at his cell phone, oblivious to her standing next to him. Her eyes wandered over him, her imagination flicking on like a lighter as she thought of spending a night with a body like his. In her experience, men like Paul were usually good in bed, from all the practice as women threw themselves at him. But you often had to prod them out of their self-induced god complex and remind them that there were two people in the bed who needed to complete things. Maeve was willing to help him out on that front.

Before he could catch her staring, she twisted her head around to the only other person in the elevator, Old Lady Deetz. The woman didn't look up from the latest copy of "Good Housekeeping" as she leaned against the wall and ignored everyone.

Maeve turned back to the front and stared at the intersection of the two elevator doors, wondering if anyone had ever gotten anything stuck in them. She had just watched a movie the night before where something happened in an elevator—

"Penny for your thoughts," Paul said, bringing her back to reality.

Her breath caught in her throat as she got lost in his deep chestnut eyes—

***

A pulsating red light flashed in front of Maeve, blotting out the image of Paul in front of her. She screamed as a thousand invisible barbs pierced her skin and lightning coursed through her veins. The shock seeped from her blood and her skin shuddered as the barbs withdrew themselves. Maeve rubbed her arms and looked around, confused.

The elevator walls had vanished. They were now in some sort of room, its walls covered in a shivering gelatinous substance. It was both translucent and murky. Emitting a soft purple glow, it seemed to be the only source of light in the room. Sinewy tendrils hung from the ceiling, swaying with an unsettling rhythm. The floor was firm and freezing. She sensed a low vibration beneath her feet.

A few feet away, much further than he had been just a second before, stood Paul. He was also rubbing his arms and staring at the wall in front of him.

Maeve turned to find Mrs. Deetz on the floor behind her.

She dropped to her knees and moved the sparse gray hair covering the old woman's face. Milky, ice-blue eyes peered up at her, unmoving. Maeve grabbed the woman's wrist, wrapping her fingers around the loose, thin skin. There was no pulse.

Paul stared at her, eyebrows raised. She shook her head and looked back down at the old woman.

"What-" Maeve began to say before someone shrieked on the other side of the jelly wall inches away from the body of Mrs. Deetz.

She stepped closer to the barrier and reached out. Before her outstretched hand could touch it, the portion of the wall in front of her solidified and separated from the rest.

The object took on a cube-like shape as it hovered inches in front of her. Maeve tried to move back, but she appeared stuck. She tried to yell, to warn Paul, but her mouth wouldn't open. She couldn't speak, couldn't even breathe. Her eyes darted to her right and she could vaguely see a similar object in front of his face.

The walls around them shook and contracted outward, as if the room had taken a deep breath and held it along with her own. Stars flickered in her vision and her body swayed. Suddenly, her breath returned to her lungs and the hold was released from her body. She staggered backward away from the object.

Both items hesitated before settling back into the wall. The smooth surface rippled until it was once again covered with the thick substance.

"What's happening?" Maeve whispered to Paul, her eyes roaming the walls around them. "What is this?"

"I don't know," he answered, "but it's not good, whatever it is."

"No shit," Maeve muttered as she shuffled toward Paul.

The floor shifted again and as she walked closer to him, and the vibration increased to a steady hum. Maeve could almost reach out and touch Paul, but a sharp pain seared through her body. It was as if her blood had become poison and was tearing her apart as it ran through her, shredding her veins along the way.

Maeve screamed and fell backward, landing closer to her original spot. The feeling immediately ceased, and she turned to her side and vomited.

"I don't think it wants us to be near each other," Paul said from across the small room.

Maeve climbed to her feet. "*I'm* okay, thanks for asking."

Paul ignored her. "It's almost.... *alive.*" He smiled as the walls rippled in front of him.

She stared at him incredulously. "How can you be *happy* about this?!"

"Don't you see? We're inside something amazing! Some sort of sentient— "

"Something that's *hurting* us. Hurting *me.*"

"You angered it," Paul said matter-of-factly.

"I— "She stopped and shook her head. "Fuck you."

Paul didn't seem to hear her as he moved backward, away from the wall. Nothing changed.

He proceeded to take small steps in every direction, testing. Maeve watched in silence, too terrified to budge from her spot.

His face fell as he stepped closer. "Nothing's happ— "

The skin on her arms bubbled and festered as if she were being boiled alive. Maeve had never known anything could feel like that.

He was close to her, eyes wide. He took several steps back, and her pain subsided.

"So that hurt you?" Paul asked.

"No shit you asshole!" Maeve screamed, "You're *fine*? Why is it only hurting *me*?!"She rubbed her arms, but the skin was smooth as if nothing had happened.

"It felt *good*." Paul grinned. "Like a massage all over my body."

"I'm so happy for you." Maeve rolled her eyes. "Now stay the fuck away from me."

"I wonder..." Paul took a half-step toward her.

Her entire body itched, and she scratched deep angry welts along her arms trying to find the source.

"Stop!"

Paul moved closer.

There was a stabbing sensation, then a ripping inside her skull. One side of the room went dark and there was a wet sensation on her cheek, something slipping down. She reached up to grab it and held it out in front of her. Maeve froze. She was holding one of her eyes. She had been born with Heterochromia; her left eye was hazel, and the right was a bright blue. She was holding the blue eye.

She looked up at Paul, not believing what was happening. His own eyes were wide and he was smiling, a sense of euphoria on his face. He shuffled back.

Her hand emptied, and she reached up, feeling two perfectly good eyes beneath her lids. The pain had ceased.

Paul shrugged. "At least it isn't permanent."

She roared as she lunged forward. Her arms were outstretched, hands reaching out to grab his throat-

She hit an invisible wall, one that seemed as if it were coated with razor-blades that had been dipped in acid. Maeve fell to the ground and crawled back to the other side of the room, every inch feeling like another razor withdrawing from her skin. A few feet, and ice replaced the acid. Back in her spot, she sat on the floor and dropped her head into her hands.

So quiet, almost discernible, she whispered, "Stay the fuck away from me... *please*."

"It's fascinating, like an orgasm ten times better than any I've ever had before." He smiled to himself and took a deep breath. He closed his eyes and touched himself, before opening them again.

"I want more."

"More? Jesus fucking fuck! You selfish prick, can't you see what's happening?"

Paul took a step and the floor rumbled. Her arms and legs vibrated with the coldness beneath her. She jumped to her feet and fell back. The sensation stopped.

He continued to move forward and her backward. They shuffled as if in a macabre dance, one he seemed to be enjoying immensely.

Maeve backed into something soft, and she spun around. It was the wall. She pushed against it, but her hands sunk up to her wrists. She pulled her hands back and examined the jelly-like substance covering them.

As she turned back around, a blur of motion caught the corner of her eye. Paul was rushing toward her. She collapsed to the ground as every bone in her body snapped at once, the cracks echoing through the small room. She thought of fireworks, the small black ones that she and her brothers used to love. Maeve screamed as Paul reached her and wrapped himself around her disjointed body.

She closed her eyes but couldn't block out the bright light seeping into her eyelids. The pain was gone, replaced by a refreshing numbness. She sighed with relief before passing out.

***

"What's that?" Maeve asked Paul, wondering if he was talking to her.

Behind him, the shine of the metallic elevator wall reflected his backside.

"I said, penny for your thoughts," Paul answered. His perfect teeth dazzled beneath his smile and his nostrils flared as if he smelled something delicious.

Her stomach coiled at the sound of his voice. Suddenly the last place in the world she wanted to be was right next to that man. Confused, she shook her head to release the thought, but it clung to her like a bad dream.

"Oh, the usual, I guess." She faked a smile and reached into her purse for her keys.

Maeve faced Mrs. Deetz, hoping to avoid any further interaction with Paul. The old woman was clutching her chest with a pained look on her face.

"Are you ok?" Maeve asked.

"Yeah, just a bit of heartburn." Mrs. Deetz smirked. "When you get old like me, nothing works the same anymore."

The elevator settled to a stop and the doors opened on her floor. Maeve rushed forward and turned to the right without saying goodbye. She wasn't sure what terrified her, but something was telling her to get the hell out of there. She opened her front door and then slammed it shut behind her, flipping the dead bolt for good measure.

That night Maeve dreamed of tightness in her body, itching like a scab. She wanted to pick at it, to grab the dead bits and tear that last connective tissue away, open the ugliness she thought might be hidden beneath. But she had a feeling it was best to leave it alone... let it heal over so she would never be able to tell where it had once broken her.

Star of San Luis

Malachi pulled back his foot and kicked, sending the coyote's bones clattering down Bluewater Highway.

"Ain't never seen no coyote at the beach before," he muttered.

"We used to have one for a pet, back when I was little," Bill said. "Maggie was the *best*."

"They're not bad eatin', either." Gideon looked at the scattered remains of the animal amid the broken, dusty chunks of asphalt. Moonlight glinted off sun-bleached bones. "Well... normally."

Bill shook his head and kept walking, followed closely by the other two men. Pet or not, he'd eat two Maggies at that point if it meant a full belly. They'd existed on nothing but dried strips of cat meat stolen from a street vendor in Dallas, and a few gallons of water bartered off a group in Houston. The water had cost Bill his grandpa's old Zippo lighter, half full of fluid. The thing only worked with every other swipe of the thumb but anything that worked even a little bit seemed to be a treasure those days.

Bill turned his head to the sky and frowned. A faint light crept up from the horizon, infecting the cool night. He scanned the dilapidated beach houses on either side of the road.

"Sun's almost up, we're going in that one." He headed toward a faded yellow house perched on stilts. It all looked as if it could tumble down with the slightest gust of wind.

"There?" asked Malachi. "Why? That blue one looks way better."

"Because, dumbass... that's where *most* people would stop."

"Yeah, 'cause it's *better*. Tell me again why we ain't going there." Gideon said.

Bill stopped and sighed before turning around to face the men, who still stood in the middle of the road. "Because that's where most people would stop. And if we don't want to be bothered, *again,* on this trip, we don't go where anyone else might find us."

"We ain't seen hide nor hair of anyone in three days," Gideon argued.

"We have to be careful, that little encounter almost cost us everything." Bill glanced at the packages.

"Oh," said Gideon.

"Yeah, *'oh'*, now make yourself fucking useful and help me carry this shit upstairs."

Bill dropped the rusted handle of the Red Radio Flyer wagon he had been pulling for the last few hours. Seemed like everyone suddenly forgot whose turn it was, so he grabbed it just to get on the damn road. He rubbed the callouses on his hands before bending to retrieve a tightly wrapped bundle from inside the wagon.

Gideon and Malachi picked up the remaining cloth-covered items and followed Bill up the stairs, through a door with a busted lock, and into the beach house.

As the men fell asleep, the sun rose.

***

When Bill opened his eyes, the sun and its scorching rays were a hazy memory in the West, disappearing with each passing minute. Bill sat on the porch, holding a few gulps of water in his mouth. He tilted his head back, slipped a slice of cat jerky past his teeth, and held it there with the water, hoping to bring back some sort of life to the poor excuse for food. It didn't work.

He swallowed the water and chewed on the meat as Gideon and Malachi joined him on the porch.

Malachi sat next to Bill and poured his own ration of water before leaning against the side of the house, licking his dry lips. "Is it up yet?"

Gideon stared off toward the night sky and rubbed his feet. The thin-soled shoes he found in a house near Pearland sat in front of him.

"Nope," Bill answered. "Not yet."

They waited.

***

Bill tried to imagine his life before everything happened, but he honestly couldn't remember a time when he wasn't staring at the sky and waiting for a star. Since he was a kid, his grandfather had told him about the new King and the star that would rise above his birth. The Child would save them all, ushering in a new way of life that didn't have them nearly starving, terrified to feel the sun on their skin. Over the years, the story had grown legs, and Bill was no longer sure how much of it was true and how much of it was them just wanting to be rescued by *anything*. Bill was now forty-five, much older than most men lived those days, and he felt every bit of it in his aching bones and stiff back. But he would have traversed three times the distance they'd come if it meant seeing the prophecies fulfilled and being able to go outside during the daytime again.

Gideon and Malachi grew up with similar stories. They had all found each other in a pub outside Oklahoma City. Bill was slouched at a table in the corner drinking a pint of hooch when Malachi walked in. Malachi was much shorter than whomever he had stolen his jeans from—they were rolled up at the ankles several times over. Everyone was thin those days, but Malachi was especially so. Looked to Bill like he wasn't much longer for this world. But he carried a package wrapped identically to the one in the wagon at his feet, so they were stuck with each other. It wasn't but a few hours later when Gideon had shown up, wearing one-piece coveralls with long sleeves. He was a little more filled out than Bill and looked like he hadn't suffered as much as everyone else. His grandpa used to say that meant he came from money, but in those days money was as useless as tits on a boar hog. Gideon must have come from one of the few remaining farms that had yet to be taken over by bandits. He carried the same wrapped package. Their pale, sun-starved faces reflected the lamplight flickering from the middle of the table where they talked over drinks, getting to know each other.

They were all following the brightest star in the sky, the Star of San Luis.

***

Bill pulled the wagon through the broken door and held the front, while Gideon grabbed the back end; they hauled it down the steps.

Bill pulled the wagon through the broken door and held the front, while Gideon grabbed the back end; they hauled it down the steps.

They dropped the wagon on the ground and walked to the road. Bill wasn't pulling that damn thing one more day. Let the other assholes help out. The prophecies never spoke of a leader among the three men, but Bill was the one with the least number of screws loose, so they had unofficially appointed him their boss. He was fine with that, as long as they kept moving forward. Kept following that star.

As they walked, the wagon rattled against loose chunks of asphalt. The bad wheel that had threatened to pop off since Houston finally gave up the fight, nearly tipping the contents onto the road.

"We're close." Bill grabbed the package he had so carefully wrapped what felt like years before. "Grab your shit, we carry 'em from here."

Malachi and Gideon didn't hesitate before picking up their items and continuing down the road after Bill. The men made for a strange sight, walking single file down a dusty, unused road in the middle of the night, but no one was around to see. They had encountered only a few people thus far and had done what they needed to do to protect their mission. It was too important to get sidetracked by a couple of mangy thieves.

Ahead of them, the road ended in a jagged hole. Next to it, an old sign hung haphazardly on a pole.

"San Luis Pass." Bill read it aloud, the only member of the three who could read.

They stared across the water at the remains of an old bridge on the other side.

"What do we do now?" Malachi asked.

Bill looked up at the sky, at their star. It seemed to shift to the left as he watched, shining brighter than he'd ever seen before.

"We go that way." He pointed at the star northeast of them.

They followed a side road toward a grouping of houses in tight lines, with narrow canals connecting each line of houses to the waters of San Luis Pass. A clattering behind them in the distance rang out through the still night.

The men froze. There were those who would have followed them to the King, to put an end to His new life. His grandpa had said those men would be from the Devil. Bill hadn't seen any devils on the road, so he wasn't so sure about that part.

"Hurry, let's get off this road," he whispered.

They shuffled quietly into the overgrown grass and weeds until they came to the first row of houses.

"It's time," a woman whispered from above.

They jerked their heads upward and pulled their knives from their belts, ready for a fight.

"Oh, put that shit away," the woman hissed. "Do you want to reach the Child or not?"

Malachi and Gideon turned to Bill with eyebrows raised. Bill squinted into the darkness but saw only a large shape at the top of the stairs. Behind her, the star shone.

He turned to the others and returned his knife to his belt, gesturing for them to do the same.

"Smart," she purred from above them. "Below me, you'll find a boat. It ain't much, but it's been waiting for you. Take it to Moody Island."

"Umm..." Bill said.

"Right, you don't know what that is," The woman rolled her eyes.

She came halfway down the stairs, her features still hidden in shadow. Her robes fluttered in an otherwise still night, and her red hair splayed out like a lion's mane. The woman pointed to the waterway behind her house and spoke to them like they were children. "Get. In. The. Boat. Then follow the canal until you hit more water. Then just go straight until you hit land. Think y'all can figure that out?"

Bill sighed. The old woman wasn't who he had imagined as being the helper on this leg of their trip, but the prophets certainly worked in mysterious ways, so who was he to question them?

Without answering, Bill carried his bundle to the back of her house where the edge of a metal boat reflected the moonlight. The other men followed.

"What a bitch," whispered Malachi once they were out of earshot of the old woman.

"Yeah, fuck her," Gideon agreed.

Bill took a deep breath. "Whatever. Let's just go."

He clutched his package close to his chest and climbed into the rusted boat, careful not to step on the wooden oars on the floor. Bill perched on the middle seat and stared at the dark spots along the bottom of the boat. Gideon followed, climbing over Bill and settling on the front seat. He glanced down.

"What are those?" He pointed to the dark places.

"Repairs," Bill said. "Let's hope they hold."

Malachi took the bench in the back. Once they were all settled, Malachi pushed off from the dock. Bill set his package at his feet, picked up the oars, and rowed.

The canal wasn't long, and they soon emerged into the pass. The water rippled, shimmering and reflecting the light from the star above them. In the distance loomed a bulky shadow with no reflection.

"That must be the island," Gideon said.

The oars splashed as Bill rowed toward the darkness ahead. They spoke only in hushed whispers as the boat sliced through the water, drawing them closer to the dark space ahead. Finally, Bill stopped rowing and looked over the edge of the metal boat into the water below. He poked at the water with the end of the oar, pushing straight down until he met resistance.

"Malachi, get out," Bill said.

"What? Why me?"

"Because I said so. It'll only come to your knees, quit bitching. Get out and push us the rest of the way to the bank."

The boat rocked as Malachi stood. He looked down at Bill with his eyebrows raised.

"Put one leg over the edge, then your other leg," Bill said. "Just don't fucking tip us over in the process."

Malachi climbed into the water and somehow managed to not dump all of them out of the boat. Bill released his breath. He was close. So close to never having to deal with those two idiots ever again. Once the tip of the boat hit the bank, Bill and Gideon carried the packages to safety on the sand before turning back and helping Malachi pull the boat further onto the beach.

They may as well have announced their arrival with trumpets as they trekked through the thick underbrush to the center of the island, but it couldn't be helped. It was pointless to do anything else, anyway, since the Mother already had to know they were close.

When Bill stopped, Malachi bumped into the back of him, and Gideon fell onto Malachi. Gideon cursed beneath his breath. It was like he was traveling with fucking idiots, but who was he to doubt who the Prophets had picked?

Before them was a circular opening about twenty feet across. In the center sat a mottled brown tent, zippered shut. In front of the tent were the remains of a fire, smoke still curling from the ashes. Empty tins of canned beans and soup lay in a pile off to the side. A soft glow emanated from the thin walls of the tent, highlighting a diminutive figure within.

Bill handed his package to Gideon and cleared his throat. He raised his arms and spoke the words he had memorized as a child:

"Holy Mother Mary, we have come to bestow gifts upon the Child. For unto us, a Child is born, unto us a Son is given, and the world will be upon His shoulders and His name will be called Wonderful, Counselor, Mighty God, Prince of Peace, the Great I Am."

The shadow inside the tent moved, and the flaps opened as the purring from the metal zipper echoed in the small space. A woman emerged and bent over to clear the opening. As she stood, her long dark hair fell to either side of her face, and her ebony skin glowed in the moonlight. The Mother was small in stature but faced the three men with her shoulders back and a fire in her eyes. A long sleeveless dress clung to her curves, not leaving much to their imagination. A small bulge revealed her stomach, still swollen from the recent birth.

Bill's jeans tightened. It had been a long while since any of them had seen a woman, especially one so beautiful.

"What is this? Why are you here?" Mary demanded.

Malachi and Gideon's eyes darted toward Bill. This wasn't the welcome they expected.

Bill, still standing with his arms outreached, hesitated. His grandfather had not prepared him for this. He lowered his arms and clutched his hands in front of his swollen crotch.

"We, uh..." He took a deep breath to instill the wonder and holiness the moment demanded. "We saw the Child's star when it rose and have come to worship him. We have gifts."

Mary looked at the bundled package in Malachi's hand and the two in Gideon's. Her eyes rose to meet Bill's and she squinted, studying him.

"You're not gonna leave until you see Him, I guess," Mary said.

"No ma'am," Bill said. "We're supposed to give him this stuff. Then we'll be gone, I promise."

"Well, the tent's too small for everyone, so I'll bring him on out if y'all want to see 'im." Mary ducked inside the tent.

Bill turned to the others. "This is it." His voice raised a few octaves, shaking with excitement.

Mary emerged from the tent holding the Child against her chest. He was wrapped tightly in a blanket made from scraps of shirts and other fabric, creating a kaleidoscope of colors.

The men dropped to their knees with their heads bowed.

"Get up," Mary said. "We don't have time for this. He's hungry and y'all came right at dinner time."

Bill, taken aback by the lack of reverence, quickly jumped to his feet. He took his package from Gideon and gestured to the men to follow. They placed the gifts at Mary's feet, and each unwrapped what he had protected so fiercely along the journey.

In front of Bill, a block of solid gold.

Near Gideon, a small pile of Frankincense clumps.

Malachi revealed a packet of Myrrh.

They looked up to Mary—still holding the Child—and waited for her to receive the gifts on behalf of their new Lord and Savior.

She laughed. Long and hard.

Mary chortled as tears flowed down her face and she struggled to catch her breath. Finally, she managed to control her laughter. "What *the fuck* is a baby supposed to do with that shit?"

"Gold, for the King," Bill stuttered.

"And Frankincense, to burn in the sanctuary," Gideon whispered.

Mary sighed and turned to Malachi. "And you?"

"Um...it's Myrrh. For..." He hesitated. "... to symbolize the bitter times in the Child's life, to heal, and to—"

"That's enough. Yeah, we're good. But thank you for stopping by." Mary turned to go back into the tent.

"But, Holy Mother," Bill said. "Can we at least look upon his face before we go?"

Mary froze and turned around slowly, hands still clutching the Baby in her arms. She eyed the three men. Her shoulders dropped and she sighed.

"There's a stump over there by the fire. I'll set him on it, and you can look if you want to."

Mary placed the Child on the hard wood and unwrapped the blanket from around his face.

The three men knelt in front of the stump and leaned forward to look upon the Holy Child. They gasped in unison.

"This isn't..." Bill said. "That... *thing*..."

Mary grabbed the Child from the stump and held him close. She glared at the men as she walked backward toward the tent.

"He's not a *thing*," she screamed. "He's a *baby*!"

Malachi and Gideon drew their hands to the knives at their waists and looked to Bill.

"It's an *abomination*. This isn't the Holy One," Bill yelled. "This is the False God. This is... the *Devil*."

At that, Malachi and Gideon drew their knives. They all knew what to do if this happened. None of them ever thought it would, they'd assumed those were old wives' tales, yet there It was, staring them in the face.

Mary backed into the tent and placed the child on a blanket inside, never taking her eyes off Bill.

"Mary, you *know*. You know what has to be done," Bill said.

Bill took a step forward. Mary's eyes darted around before landing on the closest thing at hand, a thick branch she had used to keep the edge of the tent down.

She swung it, connecting with the side of Bill's head with a loud crack. He fell to the ground, blood pouring from a split above his right ear. The knife in his hand dropped to the ground beside him. A lifetime of training flashed before his eyes, and all of it for nothing. He had failed.

***

Mary stared at the branch in her hands, then remembered the other two men standing in front of her. She swung again but missed. Malachi jumped forward, shoving the knife into her swollen belly.

Mary looked down in shock and pulled the knife out. Blood poured onto her dress and hands.

Malachi pushed her to the grass and then yelled to Gideon, "Help me hold her down!"

Before he could turn his head toward Mary, Malachi's neck spun around with a sickening crack. He fell on top of her. She struggled beneath him, her head pinned to the ground by his chest. She could see into the tent, could see the Child staring at them with knowing eyes. His small hand raised toward Malachi.

Mary wriggled free, grabbed the knife she had pulled from her stomach, and held it out in front of her toward Gideon.

"Don't move." She panted, growing weak.

To the side, Bill moaned as he tried to pull himself up.

Without hesitation, Mary threw the knife in her hand toward Gideon. It landed with a wet *schlep* into his neck. Only the alabaster handle showed against his pale skin. He fell to the ground.

Bill had climbed to his feet and stumbled, not toward her, but to the tent. To her Child.

Mary screamed and ran, eyes wild and hair flying behind her. She jumped on Bill's back, screeching and pawing at his eyes with her nails. He continued forward, blood spurting from his face and his head wound.

He ducked into the tent and raised his knife.

Mary dug her hand into the cut on his head and clenched her fist, gripping the blood-matted hair and open skin. She yanked back. He fell toward the Child on the blanket.

It was all going to be for nothing. The man would fall on the Child and surely kill him. Mary screamed as they fell together, never loosening her grip on the hole in the man's skull. They were inches from the Child when they froze.

Mary knew what was happening, the same thing that happened with the last group who tried to harm her Child.

The Child was fighting back.

Mary climbed down from the man's back while his body hung by invisible strings.

The Child gripped the edge of His blanket and giggled.

Mary grabbed him and ran from the tent. Behind her, she could hear the man's body hit the ground with a thump, then stillness. She sat by the remains of the fire, still holding the Child. A tug at her waist drew her attention to the ragged knife wound in her stomach. The surrounding skin pulled together and cinched tight. He was healing her. Again.

Mary picked Him up and held Him against her breast, pulling the top of her shirt down. He nuzzled against her, rooted around until He found her nipple, and began to feed.

He stared back at her with eyes as red as fire. The dark color had overtaken the white sclera so all that could be seen was a deep, blood red. He blinked and the sucking slowed as He grew tired.

Mary pulled Him from her breast with one arm and laid His blanket down on the grass with the other. She placed the Child on the colorful blanket and watched Him sleep until the first rays of sunlight crept through the dark. Mary pulled the sides of the blanket up and over the Child's arms and legs, covering the dry scales that consumed His skin.

"At least we'll have food for a little while." Mary eyed the bodies around them. "I'll take care of you. Always." She leaned down and nuzzled the Child before pulling away and smiling. "Until the last of the old prophets are gone."

She carried Him into the tent and placed Him on the floor. She rolled the man's body away from them and through the flap before zipping it shut.

Cat Food

Jason's bare feet shuffled against the carpet as he crept down the narrow
hallway. Holding his flip-flops in one hand, he paused at the door to his
dad and stepmom's room. Moving closer, he held his breath and put his
ear against the door. He didn't know why he tip-toed or bothered to check
on them; he could have set his watch to their nighttime routine. Once the
door closed, their joint snoring vibrated halfway across the house within
ten minutes. But that night had been different, *important*, and he wanted
to make sure they were out, but not too out. He didn't know exactly how
many sleeping pills to slip into their sweet tea at dinner that evening, and
he had erred on the side of a permanent coma over not quite asleep. It
wouldn't be any great personal loss to him if they never woke up, the two
of them deserved that and more. He'd probably have to get his own place
and ask for more hours at the restaurant, but Lou was always bugging him
to pick up shifts so that wouldn't be an issue.

Jason sighed with relief and continued down the hallway. The snoring
didn't seem quite as loud as usual, but he was pretty sure they were both
snoring. He didn't *hate* them, after all. More like an extreme aversion to
their very existence. He did, however, hate the idea of going to prison so all
in all he figured it was okay that they were still alive.

He stopped at the narrow table near the front door and grabbed his keys.
He froze as they clinked against the glass top, but nothing stirred besides

Bertha, their orange and white cat. She sashayed out of the kitchen and wound herself around his legs, purring. Jason reached down and scratched behind her ears before opening the door to the garage.

"Stay here," he whispered to Bertha, though she hadn't obeyed a single thing in her ten years of life, so he wasn't sure why he ever talked to her at all.

Back when things were still getting built around town, he had stolen a box of thick construction trash bags and hidden them in a blue plastic bin in their garage. At the time, he wasn't sure what he would need them for but his buddy Sam had said to grab them, so he did. Jason walked to the corner of the garage, the concrete cool against his bare feet. He stepped over a stack of old fence posts his dad had saved to use in the burn pit. Jason leaned down and removed the cracked plastic lid from the tub. He pulled the bags from the bin, barely glancing at the hard hats, hammers, and plastic sheeting beneath them. Jason knew he would probably never use any of the other stuff. Sam had a habit of just taking what he could, regardless of the item's usefulness to him later. And Jason had a habit of doing what Sam told him to do. The 'ole sleeping pills in the tea that night had also been Sam's idea. Sam wasn't all bad news and bossing Jason around, though. He was tough, and a good friend to have on your side when things went south. It also didn't hurt that he worked at the local animal shelter, had the keys, and knew exactly where the days' euthanized pets were stored.

Every Wednesday, Sam had to stay late with one of the local veterinarians while they euthanized all the cats and dogs no one wanted to adopt. Well, that wasn't entirely true. The shelter held the super-cute ones for a little longer than a week, along with the puppies and kittens. But never the old or aggressive ones. Those almost immediately went to the back row of kennels after intake, what the workers all called "The Farm". Because that's what every parent tells their kids. "Spot just went to live on a farm for old dogs, he's very happy there." Said with a straight, sad face, even as Old Spot's corpse stiffened in a plastic grocery bag in the freezer. Behind the peas, of course. You couldn't run the risk of little Susie finding it before trash day.

The animals on "The Farm" at the shelter were destined for that same fate, they just usually skipped the bit about hiding out in the freezer first.

Jason lifted the garage door halfway, patting himself mentally on the back that he had thought to spray WD-40 on the squeaky bits a few days before. He was tall and had to crouch low to fit beneath the metal door. He eased it down behind him. As big and as loud as it could be, it still seemed smarter than leaving through their front door. Gretchen had just purchased one of those doorbell cameras that alerted her phone when anything moved on the front porch.

He slipped his flip-flops on and walked to his car parked a few houses down. He moved it earlier when his dad took a shower and Gretchen watched TV in the living room, sipping on her fourth gin and soda.

It was a short ride to the shelter and not a cop in sight.

Jason eased onto the shoulder half a block away, turned off his car, and waited for the vet to leave. He ducked down in his seat and pulled out his phone, holding the screen low so it couldn't be seen from the road. The heat from the day still hung in the air, and he wished he could roll a window down. At least they were doing this at night when it was slightly cooler. Jason wiped small beads of sweat from his forehead then took his baseball cap off, smoothed his short blonde hair back, and put the hat back on. As he shifted in the seat, his legs separated from the leather, breaking the damp suction with a smack. He should have rolled down a window or something but didn't want to risk being seen. But it wasn't long before he looked up in time to see the vet open the front door. Her lab coat fluttered behind her as she beelined it to her car. He slid down further as her pickup truck drove by, though he knew he didn't really have to worry about her. She focused on only one thing that night: getting home, pouring herself an entire bottle of Cabernet, and watching reruns of *Friends*. She hated Wednesdays at the shelter and always ended it with that same routine. Jason knew this because back when the vet had first started, she had been talkative with Sam, even friendly. But then it slowed until she barely spoke at all as she injected Sodium Pentobarbital into the hearts of all those abandoned pets.

Once she took a right on Oak Drive, Jason turned the key in the ignition and drove toward the animal shelter. He parked next to Sam's yellow Mustang in the front parking lot and got out, slamming his door behind him.

"Hey!"

Jason looked up. Sam ran through the front doors, waving his arms and straining to get his attention without making too much noise. His compact legs were pumping. Jason was much shorter than him and stocky. He worked out every chance he could get and it showed. His shirts were always tight against his arms, but he still had trouble getting the ladies' attention. No matter how strong you were, some chicks just didn't dig a short dude. Didn't stop him from trying, though.

"No, dumbass! Park in the back! Jesus."

"That's what she said," Jason laughed.

"I'm serious, would you fuckin' go?" Sam huffed.

"The fuck was I 'sposed to know?" Jason shook his head, climbed into his car once again, and drove behind the building.

He parked and stepped out, careful not to slam his door. The thud of it closing behind him echoed in the silence. It was eerily quiet, with no animals barking, no street traffic, and no one else there besides the two of them. Jason had never been to the shelter at night and the way the woods behind the building faded into pitch black made him uncomfortable. He rushed to the back door. In and out. Sam had said they'd be in and out in less than twenty minutes.

A red chipped brick held the door open, and a shaft of light spilled out into the night. Jason shoved the brick out of the way with his foot and walked through the door, coughing. No matter how many times he visited, he would never get used to that scent. Urine, feces, and body odors from a hundred animals. Then there was the underlying aroma of bleach that, in his opinion, they could always use a little more of.

The stillness outside continued within as if an infection had seeped into the building. Normally you couldn't even wiggle a doorknob without setting off howls from every cage, but on Wednesday nights it's like they knew what had happened to their former cellmates and thought it best to lay low. They were awake, however, and aware. As he passed the open door to the kennel room, all eyes locked on Jason. Some brown, some hazel, some bright blue, and some so dark they made the hair on his arms stand up. All of them tracked his movements, not missing a beat.

During his other visits, always after hours so Sam could let him in the back door, Jason felt like a walking sausage...as if they were just waiting for their chance to devour him. But that night they didn't seem hungry or aggressive, just watchful.

"Sam?" Jason whispered into the darkness. Up ahead, a faint glow shone beneath one of the doors.

"Back here!" Sam answered from behind the door.

Jason pushed the door open and gasped.

"Shut the door, don't wanna freak out the others any more than they already are," Sam said as he shoved dead dogs and cats into black plastic bags. "These here are mine, those over there are yours."

Jason's eyes widened as he took in the pile of fur on the floor. The cold room smelled of bleach and french fries. His eyes watered from the strong cleaner. Confused, he looked around until he noticed the takeout paper sack next to Sam.

"Well, don't just stand there, grab one and start stuffing!" Sam said as he stopped to grab a handful of fries.

Jason stared at him.

"What? I got it for lunch but didn't get a chance to finish before that bitch made me go back to work." He shoved the cold fries in his mouth.

Jason scrunched up his nose and shook his head, then turned back to the bodies on the floor. "I brought the bags you told me to…"

"I found these in the back," Sam interrupted.

"Ok." Jason pulled a bag from the roll on the table, opened it, and shook it out. He looked at the dead animal closest to him. It was a black cat, just like Raven, the one he used to have before they got Bertha. Raven had been killed by a dog on the sidewalk in front of their house. Jason had been the one to find her on his way home from school that day. She was stiff by then, and he never forgot those cold, dead eyes. He looked down at the cat, still holding the plastic in his hands and not moving. Jason knew it wasn't Raven, couldn't have been. But the resemblance….

"Dude, we don't have all night!" Sam grunted as he tried to pull the wide plastic strings at the top of another bag. A dog's leg stuck out, preventing it from closing. Sam shoved it back down and tied a knot with the strings. "What a pain in the ass." He wiped the sweat off his forehead with the sleeve of his shirt and reached for the next one.

By the night's end, Jason had packed up five dogs and eight cats, and Sam had packed six dogs and ten cats.

"I'm not sure this adds up," Jason said as he looked at Sam's stack, then back again at his own.

"I did most of the work and it's my ass on the line, anyway. I think it's more than fair," Sam grunted as he hefted one of Jason's bags onto a cart.

One by one, they loaded Jason's haul into the trunk of his car. The night remained still, only the crunching of their feet on the gravel and the thunk of the animals landing in the trunk breaking the silence.

Sam stopped and leaned against the back of the building. He pulled a roach from his pocket, straightened the bent ends, and lit it.

Jason glared at him. There were still three bags sitting on the ground in front of his trunk. "Really? You think *now* is a good time for that?"

"What? I helped with the others. Want me to do everything?"

Jason closed the trunk and pulled his keys from his pocket.

"Where do you think you're going?"

He reached for the door handle and rested his hand on it. "Home"

Sam tossed his keys to Jason.

"Pull my car around so we can load mine up. I wanna finish this. That bitch won't let me take smoke breaks anymore."

Jason sighed and replied, "Sure, why not? Did she *ever* let you smoke that?"

Sam smiled. "She never asked, I never said."

When he returned, Sam had gone back into the building and the door had once again been propped open with the brick.

Jason backed the car up next to his own, pulled the keys from the ignition, and stepped out of the car.

"Sam?" His voice echoed through the darkness ahead. Something rustled in the trees behind him, and he went through the door and closed it without looking back. Jason intended to creep again past the doorway to the kennel room. He couldn't handle all that...*quiet*, and those eyes. But he stopped and peeked around the corner when a high-pitched whimper echoed from the room. There, in the middle of the floor in the most adorable pile of brown fluff, sat a small puppy. Large dark eyes stared at Jason as he tip-toed across the room. A black Labrador shifted in a cage to his right, eyeing him but remaining quiet. On his left, a white pit bull mix chased something in his sleep, with small whimpers and his legs twitching as he ran into the unknown.

Jason reached the puppy and bent down to pick her up. She was heavier than he thought she'd be. Just solid puppy fatness. She settled into the crook of his arm with a sigh. Her fur was fluffy and brown with black streaks throughout. For a moment, he contemplated tucking her inside his jacket and taking her home.

"Dude, what're you doing?" Sam called from the doorway. "Put it back and help me finish this, I gotta meet Rudy in a few to get some more grass."

"Where am I supposed to put her?" Jason looked around as he scratched behind the puppy's ears.

Sam pointed to an empty cage, the door still closed and locked tight. "Shove it back in there. It must have crawled through the bars."

Jason opened the metal door and placed the puppy onto a tattered red blanket. He closed and locked the door and stood up.

"How you gonna keep her from gettin' out again?"

"I don't give a fuck, now come on," Sam said as he walked to the rear of the building.

Jason looked around the room, spotted a wooden board in the corner, and placed it in front of the bars of the cage, covering the bottom half.

"There, now you're kind of safe," he whispered.

She waddled toward the bars and looked up at him, whimpering. He locked eyes with her before sighing and standing back up. Jason walked back outside, where Sam had already loaded two of the pets into his trunk.

"'Bout damn time, you done fuckin' around?" he grunted as he picked up a bag.

"I went in looking for you, ass-wipe."

"I had to take a shit." Sam looked at him before reaching for another. "That all right with you?"

Jason rolled his eyes and helped him load the rest of the animals in silence.

***

Jason backed his car into the driveway and turned the ignition off. He sat in the darkness, his stomach rumbling with hunger. Their dinner that night had been sparse, as usual. A few veggies from his dad's garden in the backyard, sautéed in a little bit of water to keep them from sticking to the pan. Oil was expensive so they tried to ration what little they had, saving it for the company that never came over and special occasions that never happened.

Jason hoped the sleeping pills were still doing the trick, and briefly considered a world where they never woke up. He would have finally gotten revenge for his mother's "accident." The state couldn't prove it in court, but Jason and his older sister, Carrie, were pretty sure their dad had been responsible for their mother's death.

Carrie was twenty years older than him and had been the mom in his life ever since his own died. Jason's conception had been the unsuccessful "save our marriage by having a child" child. The divorce had finalized three days after he turned two years old, and their dad claimed he met Gretchen a few months later when he skipped an AA meeting to go to a strip club. She had headlined that night, and her golden tassels mesmerized their dad to the point of him proposing that very night in the parking lot when she got off work. That had been their official love story, anyway. Carrie had never believed that bit and liked to tell Jason that their bond was probably sealed in a private VIP room in the back of the club while he and their mom were still married. An extremely bitter custody dispute followed. Carrie and Jason had taken their mom's side, of course, which only served to motivate their dad more to get custody of them. His dad was a classic narcissist; not wanting them because he cared, but because he wanted to *win*. He ended up with custody by default when their mom had been killed.

Their mom had taken their dog, Nico out for their usual walk. She would take him out every evening after they ate dinner, like clockwork. Nico was an extremely high-energy dog and if he didn't get his walk in, he would become unbearable in the evenings, bringing his toys to everyone and whining until they played with him. Their mom had been in the middle of crossing the street at the corner of Wilkins and Polk when a car (or a van, or a truck... they never found out who did it) plowed into her and Nico. The cops said she probably didn't feel anything. Both had died instantly. Nice and tidy. Convenient.

Their dad had acted shocked and sad at the news, even crying a few fake tears in front of the cops. Carrie and Jason's tears were real.

He eased the garage door back open and pulled a string to a light hanging from the ceiling. The bulb clicked on, illuminating one side of the garage. His stomach grumbled again, and a sharp pain caused him to wince, surprising him. It had been a while since he felt hungry. He did all the time toward the beginning but then, like everyone else, he became used to it and noticed it less and less. Hungry was just what they all *were*. It wasn't only his family, it was everyone. Carrie and her husband, Sam and his family, and all their friends and neighbors. The whole country was hungry. Jason rubbed his stomach, took a deep breath, and opened the trunk of his car.

Thanking Sam for being able to get them the stuff while it was still fresh, he pulled each of the bags from his car and laid them next to the deep freeze against the far wall of the garage. Once full of his dad's deer and hog meat, the freezer had sat empty for years. The day before, Jason had grabbed it by the edge and shifted it away from the wall with a grunt. He blew away the dust, found the old cord, and said a quick prayer to any god who would listen as he plugged it back in.

Jason held his breath while opening the top of the freezer. A blast of stale, cold air hit him in the face, and he smiled. The old girl still worked. He jogged to the car and closed his trunk. He glanced up and down the street, but he needn't have worried. No one was out on that hot summer night. No one was out much anymore at all. The less you moved around, the fewer calories you burned, and they were all thin enough. He eased the garage door down with a soft thud and walked to the pile of bags. As he dropped each animal down into the freezer, he thought of that puppy again and what each of the dead things looked like when they were young. Were they sweet? Did someone love them and take care of them? He shook off the thoughts. He knew it wasn't optimal. It wasn't what anyone *wanted* to do. But it was what had to be done and he knew once he talked to his dad and Gretchen, and Carrie and her husband Manny, that they would agree. He had saved them all; they had to see that.

He closed the top of the freezer and picked up the last bag. It didn't seem as heavy as the others, a perfect specimen to begin with. Jason opened the door to the house and peeked toward his dad's room down the hall. The door remained closed, and no light showed from beneath it. He breathed a sigh of relief and quickly walked to his room. Beneath a blanket, on the far side of his bed out of sight of the door, sat an ice chest. A plastic sack full of ice from Wick-Mart sat in the bottom. He had prepared it all earlier before his dad got home from work. Jason placed the bagged animal on top of the ice with a crunch, closed the lid, and covered it again with the blanket.

Piece of cake.

He smiled at how smoothly everything had gone as he headed toward the kitchen.

Bertha waited on the other side of his door and jerked back from him as he entered the hallway. She sniffed the air around him, laid her ears flat against her head, and hissed before running into the kitchen. The plastic square of her cat door flapped against its frame before settling to a close.

"Whatever. Be happy it ain't you," Jason said.

In better days, their kitchen had been bright and cheerful. But the sunflower-yellow walls had faded to a murky tan, the table in the middle of the room wobbled no matter how many things you wedged beneath the legs, and the plastic backing on the chairs had all cracked, scratching the shit out of anyone who wore shorts. He opened the fridge and stared at the empty spaces where food used to be. Leftovers had become a thing of the past. A few ears of corn and some squash sat on the middle shelf, and off-brand cokes and Miller Lite were on the bottom shelf. Next to the beer sat an unidentifiable casserole from Mrs. Billie Jean down the street sat on the middle shelf. That would be tomorrow's dinner, he knew, and it looked disgusting. Rumor had it that Billie Jean ate canned cat food, and he had no desire to consume anything that came from her kitchen.

He turned away from the fridge empty-handed and decided to take a shower before he did anything else. Bertha was right, he reeked.

***

Carrie chopped vegetables for soup when she had to stop and look up at the television. At the time, she didn't even know why she tuned in at that exact moment. Perhaps between each crunchy slice of carrot and the thud of the knife against the wooden chopping board, her subconscious had picked up on something different. A change in tone, maybe, or the way someone could ask a question, and even as the other person responded with a "what's that?" their brain had a chance to catch up and they already knew the answer.

"Turn that up," she gestured toward the TV with the knife.

Her husband Manny, sitting on the couch while half-watching the news and half-playing on his phone, reached for the remote. Their baby daughter, Olivia, snoozed in a pink bouncy seat on the floor in front of him. She had her father's dark complexion and her mother's height. Her feet dangled off the end of the seat, one in a frilly green sock and the other bare. The sock lay discarded beneath her.

An exterior shot of the Brazoria County Animal Shelter filled the screen, then the reporters cut to a traffic jam on I-10.

"That son-of-a-bitch did it."

Manny had already returned to his phone. He looked up and asked, "What?"

"Jason. He broke into the animal shelter." Carrie finished chopping and tossed the vegetable scraps into a bag before putting them in the freezer. "What a dumbass."

She dropped the cut carrots into a pot of water on the stove with a splash and turned the dial until it clicked on.

"Are you serious? I thought he was just kidding."

"Yeah, I'm serious. *He* was serious. He's hungry, Manny. What do you expect?"

"I expect him to eat what the rest of us have to eat. What makes him so special anyway? We're *all* hungry." Manny stood up from the couch and stretched. He glanced at the baby before joining Carrie in the kitchen. "Speaking of eating, when's lunch gonna be ready?"

"When it's ready." Carrie glared at him before pulling her phone from her back pocket and pulling up her little brother's number. He answered after the first ring.

"Jason? What the hell did you do? Are you a fucking idiot?"

She paused to listen.

"Okay."

"But-"

"You can't just-"

"Are you gonna let me fuckin' talk?!"

Carrie stared at her phone in disbelief. "The asshole hung up on me!"

"Easy, you're gonna wake Ollie," Manny said gesturing to the sleeping baby. "And I don't know why you're freaking out, it's not our problem."

"His problems *are* our problems, Manny. What do you think Dad and Gretchen are gonna do when they find out? Whose couch is he gonna have to sleep on?" She jabbed her finger toward their living room. "Ours."

"It wouldn't be the first time." Manny shrugged.

"It's illegal, Manny, and *gross*. And stop calling her Ollie, her name is Olivia."

***

He knew he shouldn't have told that bitch. Of course, she wouldn't think it was a good idea, she'd been shitting on his plans since their mom died and she crowned herself "Supreme Mother." God, she needed to get off his back. Jason didn't even understand why she had her panties all in a wad, it's not like he kidnapped the neighbor's pets or microwaved Bertha. He wasn't a monster, for fucks' sake. He just took what was gonna be trash anyway. The unwanted.

Jason dropped his phone on top of his gray comforter and stared at the ceiling. He followed the fan's slow movement above him until the circles blurred. He wasn't planning on getting up that early but thanks to Carrie, his bladder also screamed at him. He swung his legs over the edge of his bed and cracked his door open. The empty hallway loomed in front of him. His dad yelled at him whenever he wore his boxers around the house, but there was no sign of him or Gretchen. Both had already gone to work. Jason shuffled barefoot down the hall to the bathroom wearing nothing but his red plaid boxers.

He loved those moments when he had the whole place to himself. He and Sam had talked about moving out and getting a place together, but they hadn't made any actual plans yet.

He left the bathroom and walked toward the kitchen. Usually, his dad left a little coffee in the pot for him, but that morning it had already been rinsed out and laid upside-down on the drying mat.

"Assholes," Jason muttered as he grabbed a coke from the fridge. The least they could do was leave him the rest of the coffee.

He plopped down on the couch, switched on the TV, and then remembered his phone still lying on his comforter in his bedroom. Local weather filtered down the hallway from the living room and Jason grabbed his phone and hurried back. The Channel 12 weather chick looked hot, he never minded watching her.

By the time he sat down, they had already returned to the main news anchors. Jason sighed and checked his notifications on his phone, only half listening to the news reports. He was scrolling through Instagram when the words "local animal shelter" blurted from the TV. His head snapped up and he dropped his phone on the couch cushion.

"Oh shit," he whispered.

There it was, clear as day, the shelter he and Sam had just left the night before. Apparently, the staffers noticed the dead animals missing when they got there that morning and reported it to the police.

"Shit, shit, shit..."

Keeping his eyes on the screen, he felt around the couch for his phone and brought it up in front of him. He pulled up the text messages between him and Sam, but there wasn't anything new. Maybe Sam still slept.

Jason called him. "Pick up... Pick up..."

Eyes still on the TV, he tuned out the ringing phone and listened. They were saying Sam was a "person of interest." He bet anything that bitch vet ratted him out, said he had stayed behind after she left, and that he probably did it. But they also said they were still investigating and couldn't get in touch with Sam. Jason knew what that was like. The ringing stopped as the call went to voicemail.

"Sam, answer the fucking phone! Call me back when you get this."

The news changed to a ribbon-cutting ceremony at some bullshit place no one cared about. Jason thought about going over to Sam's house, but what if the cops were watching it? What if they were over there right then and saw Jason had called Sam's phone? He needed to lay low for a bit, no one had to know he had been a part of it. Carrie was the only one that knew they were considering doing what they did but as much as she liked to bitch at him, she'd never turn him in. He knew Sam didn't blab. He was pretty smart that way. No one said *Jason's* name on the news.

For the moment, he felt safe.

He had planned to cook the meat from the ice chest in his room and have it ready on the table when his dad and Gretchen got home from work. It would be harder to argue against him with the food right there in front of their faces, presented just like beef, hog, or deer. He wasn't sure what dog or cat tasted like, or which meat it came closest to even *looking* like. He read somewhere that human meat tasted like a combination of beef and pork. They didn't call it "Long Pig" for nothing, he guessed.

He walked back down the hallway where Bertha sat in front of the door to his dad's room, staring at the white wooden door. She turned to watch him walk by but never budged from her spot.

"Whatever, you're fuckin' weird," Jason said as he continued to his room.

He pulled on a pair of jeans and a t-shirt, then opened the ice chest. The thick plastic made it harder to cut through than he thought, which he supposed was a good thing. No drippage. Jason pulled a pocketknife from his nightstand and cut into the bag. He hadn't noticed the night before whether it was a dog or a cat, and if he was going to have to cut it up, he needed to have an idea of what he had gotten himself into.

The plastic parted to reveal the head of a cat. A formerly white, now something cold and gray, cat. He twisted the piece of cut plastic around until he couldn't see the animal anymore and closed the lid of the ice chest. Jason went back into the hallway, passing Bertha again on his way to the living room. She didn't turn that time but continued staring at the bedroom door in front of her. Jason shook his head and plopped down on the couch.

He grabbed the remote, put a baking show on even though he never baked a day in his life and didn't plan to, and pulled his phone from his pocket. He liked the accents of the contestants and liked watching the stuff they came up with. Maybe one day he'd bake. Either way, it made for good background noise as he searched the internet for how to skin and clean a raccoon. He figured it was the closest to a cat there could be, and no one pulling his search history later would accuse him of eating a cat.

"Hopefully there really is more than one way to skin a cat," Jason chuck-led to himself.

The sun lowered in the sky, shining through the big window in the living room as it continued its descent.

He regretted not taking a bigger interest in going hunting with his dad all those years back when they still could do things like that. All that remained then were fishing and crabbing and even though they lived on the coast, the Texas Wildlife and Fisheries Department closely patrolled everything from the bayous to the bays. With so many looking to fish for their meals, the risk of overfishing increased, and then they'd all be fucked. They still allowed you to buy a fishing license but severely restricted the amount you could legally bring home, and his dad always hit his limits too soon. They would greedily eat fish for every meal before it ran out, instead of rationing it like Jason always said they should do. He thought maybe they didn't trust him not to steal it again from the freezer when they weren't looking.

***

Carrie and Manny had worked nights for as long as they could remember. They were both dispatchers for the Clute Police Department, and the Captain had been nice enough to put them on the same schedule. Otherwise, it would have been nearly impossible to spend any time together. If they had to pay for a real babysitter, they would have been on separate shifts as soon as Olivia was born. But luckily, Manny's mom had offered to watch the baby to help them save on costs. Still fuming from the situation with her brother, they dropped Olivia off at her grandmother's and drove to work that night in silence.

"I mean, what was he thinking!" she pounded on the steering wheel with her hand.

"I don't really see what the big fuckin' deal is, Care. We're not the ones eating it," Manny said.

"I know, I just... He's my little brother, Manny! And he could get arrested for this! What would that look like for us?"

"That's what you're worried about? What everyone at work will think of you if your brother is arrested?" Manny turned his head back to the road and shook it in disbelief.

"No." Carrie raised her voice. "Of course, I'm worried about him getting in trouble but don't be naïve, Manny. You know they'll talk."

"No more than they talked when Sgt. Lopez's wife got that DWI. That's the benefit of a small town, you can sweep that shit under the rug. Now, aren't you glad we didn't apply to Houston when they were hiring?"

"Just shut up." Carrie turned the radio up and drove the rest of the way to work in silence.

When they arrived, it seemed business as usual. No one talked about the break-in at the shelter. It wasn't relevant to anyone else but Carrie and Manny. To the rest of the dispatchers, it remained a small line item at the end of the blotter from the day shift. Nothing of interest.

Halfway through their shift, however, all of that changed.

***

The cast iron pan sizzled as it cooked the cat meat, and Jason's stomach wrenched in pain, remembering meals past. Meals he never thought he'd get a chance to eat again. Surely once they smelled it, his dad and Gretchen would be eager to eat and thankful he had helped out. Jason pulled a piece from the pan, placed it on a cutting board, and dug around in the drawer for their old meat thermometer. He wiped the dust from it and popped it into the meat. There wasn't a temperature marker for "cat", so he went with the beef guidelines. Jason always liked his steaks on the rare side and figured cats and dogs couldn't be much different. He pulled the thermometer from the meat and a few drops of blood oozed up from the small hole.

"Perfect," he said, before cutting off a bite-sized piece and popping it into his mouth.

"Ohhhhhh, this is *it*," Jason moaned as the juices ran down the back of his throat, the charred edges rough against his tongue. He would have preferred to cook it in butter, but all dairy products were also off-limits.

He ate the rest of the meat on the cutting board, knowing he still had plenty to cook for the others. Jason seared the rest of the meat with a full belly, enjoying the scents wafting around the kitchen without the growls and pain from his stomach. He glanced at his watch; it was almost time for his dad and Gretchen to get home. He quickly pulled the rest of the meat from the pan and let it rest on the cutting board before slicing it and placing it on three plates. They still used his mom's dish set, tan plates with brown plants and flowers swirling around the edges. If Gretchen had known they were his mom's plates, she would have broken them all years before. She just assumed his dad had picked them up and joked about his shitty taste in dishes.

Jason set each one down on the table in front of their usual seats. He pulled a fork and knife from a drawer and put one on each side of the plates. He tilted his head and looked at the arrangement before moving them both to the right side. He had no idea what the proper layout looked like, but it seemed pretty good to him. Jason plopped down in his usual spot. They would be home any minute.

He looked at the table and smiled.

***

"271 to Dispatch."

"Come in, 271."

Carrie glanced at Manny in the chair next to her and wiggled her eyebrows. There had been a running joke that Officer Barton (271) had a crush on Manny ever since Barton drank too much at the Christmas party and lingered a little too long hugging Manny goodbye.

Manny rolled his eyes and turned back to the display panel in front of his station. The dispatch room consisted of a semi-circle of monitors, computers, keyboards, and microphones with two rolling chairs inside. Typically, one dispatcher answered the 911 line and the other handled the police, fire, and EMS calls. Though that never really mattered, everyone helped out where they could on those rare nights when the shit hit the fan.

"10-38 at the corner of Plantation and Highway 288, northbound. 10-28 on Texas GKA-01Z2. Yellow Ford Mustang."

"10-4," Carrie answered, her brow furrowed. Sam drove a yellow Mustang. She swallowed and sat up straight as she entered the license plate into the database and waited, hoping Jason wasn't with him. The panel to her left finished searching, showing the results on the small black screen.

"Ugh, it *is* him," Carrie said to Manny before pressing the button. "Dispatch to 271, Plate comes back to a Sam Dorren. 10-69?"

Carrie waited while the officer moved toward his patrol car so Sam couldn't hear the radio. Manny turned to listen.

"Dispatch, go ahead."

"Owner possibly involved in a breaking and entering on the 23rd of this month. Wanted for questioning by Lake Jackson PD."

"10-4."

Carrie chewed on her fingernail and waited for Barton to confirm it was Sam driving the Mustang. Manny whispered, "Of course it's him, it's his car. I bet Jason's there, too."

"Shut up," Carrie hissed at her husband before the radio crackled, interrupting them.

"271 to Dispatch, 10-27 on TX 686368382."

"10-4, standby."

Manny read the screen over Carrie's shoulder after she punched in the driver's license number and whistled. "I told you."

Carrie sighed. "Whatever, at least Jason isn't with him."

"Dispatch to 271-" The radio cut off with a squeal.

"Dispatch, subject fleeing on foot eastbound on Plantation, requesting backup," Officer Barton huffed into the radio as he ran.

"10-4. Attention all units, assistance requested at Plantation and 288. Subject Sam Dorren fleeing on foot, eastbound on Plantation, white male, 6'3", approx. 250lbs. Brown hair," Carrie spoke into the microphone before releasing the button. She put her elbows on the desk and laid her head on her hands, closing her eyes and taking a deep breath.

The radio squawked again, and Officer Barton yelled out between breaths as he ran, "Blue jeans, white hoodie!"

Carrie looked up and pressed the button. "10-4."

She knew she didn't need to bother relaying the description any further, as two other units announced that they were en route and had heard the descriptions.

Carrie told Manny to call Jason while she arranged for a tow truck to pick up the Mustang. The officers kept searching but never caught up with Sam.

***

Jason watched his phone ring until it went to voicemail. He had no desire to talk to Manny or Carrie. He knew what they were gonna say and had grown tired of hearing it. Carrie had acted like his mom his entire life, and sometimes it just got old. He didn't need a mom or a bossy sister. The phone rang again, still Manny. He ignored it again.

The wooden chair legs screeched against the floor as he pulled back from the table and headed toward the bathroom. As he turned the corner into the hallway, he saw Bertha still sitting near the door to his dad's bedroom.

"Hey, girl. You still mad at me?" Jason knelt and reached for the cat, clicking his tongue. "Come here, girl."

Bertha sauntered toward him, her tail held high, twitching back and forth. As she came closer, he noticed a strange odor in the hallway. He reached out to pet Bertha and looked around for the source of the smell but couldn't see anything.

"Did you bring another mouse into the house, girl?" But it wasn't quite like a dead rodent's stench... "Or did you have an accident outside the litter box?"

She pulled back from him as if indignant and ran toward the kitchen. Jason jumped up and grabbed her before she could get to the dinner table. He didn't think she'd know the chunks of meat were from another cat but didn't want to risk her snatching any of it off their plates before dinner time.

"You can just wait in here until after we eat," he said as he tossed Bertha into his bedroom and shut the door.

After he used the bathroom, he walked back down the hallway to the kitchen. The smell seemed stronger in the hallway, but he didn't have time to investigate it further. He wanted to see the look on his dad and Gretchen's face when they saw the food, so he hurried back to the table.

The minutes ticked by and he ignored four more phone calls from Manny and three from Carrie. Jason kicked his flip-flops off into the corner and looked at the clock again. They were extremely late. He rolled his eyes and sighed. They probably went to the bar and then to see a movie after work. Sometimes they did that without telling him. When he complained about it, their answer had always been, "Well you're hardly ever home anyway, we didn't think you cared."

He *didn't* care but still liked to know things.

"Fuck it," Jason said as he picked up a knife and fork and cut off a small piece of meat. He chewed on it, rolling it around in his mouth trying to savor the feeling. It had been a while since he'd had anything so delicious. Before he realized it, he had devoured his food and washed it all down with a coke. He crumpled the can and tossed it into the trash as his phone rang again. Sighing, he glanced at the device expecting to see his sister's name but was surprised to see Sam's.

"Shit," he muttered, realizing he had stopped trying to get a hold of Sam earlier. Some friend he was... Jason picked up the phone.

"Hey, I'm in some trouble," Sam said, breathing hard.

"Yeah, I saw. What the fuck are we gonna do?" Jason asked.

"No...not just the news." Sam coughed. "The cops have my car, man."

"What? What did you do? You okay?" Jason grabbed the plates and tossed them in the fridge. He held the phone between his ear and his shoulder and shoved his flip-flops back on.

"Nah, man. You at your house? I'm here in the back. Didn't wanna knock since your dad's home."

"Dad isn't-" Jason walked to the front door and stopped. He tilted his head, waiting to hear his dad's truck pull into the driveway.

"Dude come on. I'm kind of in a crisis, here."

"Be right there." Jason shrugged and ran to the back door. He had to jerk on the door handle a few times before it would open. The house settled depending on the seasons and in the summer, the back door stuck. He stepped onto the porch and eased the door closed. If his dad had just pulled in, he didn't want him to know he was outside with a fugitive. He squinted into the darkness.

"Where are you?" Jason whispered.

"Over here and keep it down!" Sam hissed from a corner of the yard.

Jason walked to the corner and finally spotted Sam standing beneath an oak tree by the back fence. Sam still wore his clothes from the day before and he stunk like rotten food.

"Dude, shower much?" Jason waved his hand in front of his face.

Sam looked around him toward the house. "Got any of that meat left?"

"Meat?" Jason's brow furrowed in confusion.

"From yesterday. The dogs and cats, man. The meat." Sam said as he covered a cough with his hand. The hand almost glowed in the moonlight, pale and bright. His eyes were wide and his face glossed with sweat.

Jason stared at his friend. Sam shifted his weight from leg to leg and scratched his head. When he pulled his hand away, thick bunches of his hair came with it, leaving a bald patch. Sam didn't seem to notice as he repeated, "Do you? Do you?"

"Yeah, of course. What, I'm gonna eat it all in a day?" he laughed, trying to lighten the mood, but Sam walked around him and headed toward the house.

Jason backed up and put his hand on Sam's chest. "What are you doing? You can't go in there, you're all over the news and Dad'll turn you in. You *know* he will."

"So, we'll take care of 'im." Sam pushed against Jason's hand, his eyes glued to the back door of the house.

"Take care of him? The fuck is wrong with you, man?" He grabbed the front of Sam's shirt to hold him still.

Sam flung his head around, inches from Jason. "I'm just so *hungry*. Come on...share." His rancid breath blew into Jason's face, and he dropped his head and gagged. Jason opened his eyes, and his dinner tickled the back of his throat as he looked at Sam's shirt. Vomit, dirt, and a dark thick sludgy mixture of the two covered the shirt.

He let go of his friend and jumped back. "What the fuck, man?"

"Forget it, I'll go back to the source. Get more there anyway. Fuck you." Sam said as he jogged toward the trees at the edge of the yard. He didn't look back as he came to the chain-link fence, grabbed the metal bar on the top, and hurled himself over. He landed on the other side and kept running.

"What the actual..." Jason said to himself. He looked down at his hands. They were dirty and smelled awful, the puke and dirt all over Sam's shirt had left remnants on his hands. He walked back into the house and washed them three times in the kitchen sink, just to be on the safe side.

Jason turned from the sink and had to grab the back of a chair to steady himself. The room spun around him, and everything seemed distorted as if he had looked through a thick layer of plastic wrap. He touched his forehead and thought it felt warm but couldn't be sure.

"I don't feel so hot," Jason whispered as everything went dark and he slumped to the floor.

***

Carrie screeched into the driveway of her dad's house, threw the car into park, and jumped out. Manny ran after her toward the front door.

"Jason!" They banged on the wooden door with both fists. "Jason!" Her idiot brother was probably asleep, but his car in the driveway proved his presence at the house.

Carrie fumbled in her pocket for her keys and unlocked the door. A powerful odor punched her in the chest and they both coughed and covered their noses and mouths with the front of their shirts. The front hall seemed quiet, and Bertha was nowhere in sight. The cat always greeted Carrie at the door when she would visit; Carrie did half-raise her, after all.

"Jason?!" Carrie yelled, the sound slightly muffled by her t-shirt.

"Where is everyone?" mumbled Manny.

She turned the corner into the kitchen and gasped, the shirt dropping from her face. Jason lay in a heap on the floor. His head and shoulders leaned against the oven door and his mouth hung open. He looked terrible. She dropped to his side and shook his shoulders. Manny stood over them, peering down.

"Umph," Jason mumbled as he opened his eyes.

Carrie exhaled, happy he could breathe. She screamed into his face as she continued to shake him. "Jason! What happened? Are you okay?"

"What the fuck, man?" Manny said.

Jason managed to pull away from his sister in time before leaning over and throwing up onto the kitchen floor. He sat up and wiped his mouth with his shirt sleeve.

"What, are you sick?" Carrie scooted away from him, bumping into Manny behind her. Manny stumbled backward as Carrie sat on the floor.

"Sorry," she said in Manny's direction, eyes still locked on Jason.

Jason turned to Manny, then Carrie. He looked confused, like he didn't recognize them. "Sam..."

"That asshole is nothin' but trouble, I told you a hundred times-"

"What time is it?" Jason asked, looking around for the clock on the wall in the kitchen.

"Six-thirty in the morning, we just got off our shift," said Carrie.

"What-"

"I just want you to tell me why the fuck you think you can just break into places and now your best friend is getting arrested, do you know what this is going to look like for me when they find out? And they're gonna find out, it's just a matter of time-" Carrie screamed.

"Shut up!" Jason shouted, holding his head in his hands, "Shut the fuck up for a fucking minute. My head is killing me and your yelling isn't helping."

He looked up at her and said, "Carrie," as if he were just recognizing her.

"You can worry about being sick later. Right now I'm trying to keep you out of jail. Do you know that asshole ran from the fucking cops?" Carrie stood up and grabbed a paper towel from the roll on the counter. She ran cool water over it, then leaned down and pressed it to Jason's forehead.

"What? When?" Jason looked around the kitchen.

"Earlier this evening, she was actually on the radio when it happened. They're looking for him and eventually you, I'm sure. Was there a surveillance camera at the animal shelter?" Manny said.

"I don't know. I don't think so. Sam said he took care of it."

"At least that dumbass did one thing right." Carrie shook her head and stood, reaching toward Jason. "Can you stand up? What hurts?"

"Yeah." Jason ignored her outstretched hand and lifted himself off the floor. He then dropped into a chair with a thud and put his hands on the table as if to steady himself. "Everything hurts."

"Should we go to Urgent Care?" Manny asked, looking at Carrie.

"No, stop worrying. I'm okay. Just a bug. Probably got it from Sam, he looked fuckin' awful. I'll sleep it off-"

"Wait, what? You saw Sam? When?" Carrie yelled, her voice raising with each word.

"Calm your tits. He just stopped by for a second." Jason glanced at the clock in the kitchen. "A few hours ago, I guess. I don't know where he went."

Carrie huffed and sat down across from her brother. She waited until he looked at her before saying, "This is serious, Jason."

"She's right," Manny agreed.

"I *know* that."

"Do you? Because from where I'm sitting, it looks like just another day for you. You never give a shit about anything," Carrie yelled.

Jason stood up and went to the fridge. "If you're gonna yell at me some more, is it okay if I eat while you're doing it? I'm starving."

Carrie stared at Manny, waiting for him to come to her defense. Manny shrugged. "You *are* yelling."

Jason pulled the two plates out and set them on the counter. He put one in the microwave before turning to his sister and brother-in-law.

"Hungry?"

"Always," Carrie smiled. She stared at the other dish still sitting on the counter and her eyes narrowed. She stood up and went toward the food. "What..." she jabbed her finger into the top of the meat, "... is that?"

"Your dinner. Definitely yours now, since you put your grubby hands all over it. Y'all can share." Jason pulled his plate from the microwave, put theirs in, and pressed the buttons.

"Is that..." she scrunched her face up, "...a dog?"

"No fuckin' way I'm eating that," said Manny.

"No...of course not," Jason answered before smiling. "It's a cat."

He smiled that mischievous grin that had gotten him out of most things when they were younger. Carrie could never stay mad at him long. He grabbed three forks from a drawer and tossed them onto the table.

"Ugh, how did I know you were gonna say that..." Carrie rolled her eyes as he sat down at the table.

"Just try it, okay? Isn't that what Mom used to always say? You have to at least try it."

The microwave beeped and Carrie pulled the food out. Steam wafted toward her, and she closed her eyes and breathed in. "Ahh man, I miss this." Carrie smiled as she sat down. She picked up the fork and pointed it at her brother. "I'm just gonna pretend it's beef."

Manny pulled the chair out next to her and grabbed the remaining fork. "I guess we're doing this. Let me get in there, too."

They ate in silence, the three of them enjoying a meal they thought they'd never have again. With each bite, Jason ate faster and faster, until he shoveled the food into his mouth, barely chewing before he swallowed.

"Easy. Slow down or you'll get sick," Carrie said.

"I'm just so *hungry*," Jason said as he wiped his finger across the plate to get the last few bits of juice. He popped his finger in his mouth and rolled his eyes. "So. Good."

Carrie and Manny laughed. It felt good to laugh, felt good to feel normal for just a few minutes at least. It seemed like ever since the virus surfaced, it was all anyone could talk about.

They thought it first appeared at a meat market in Brazil, but no one could prove it. It then quickly infiltrated wildlife, showing up in deer and hogs. It wasn't like anything anyone had ever seen before. It was fucking *brutal*. Hunters were finding animal corpses covered with a sticky yellow film like it had oozed from their pores. Beneath the film, craters of skin had sizzled away until all that remained were hooves, antlers, or tusks. Their dad had come upon one in the early stages and watched it happen, but no one believed him until the official reports came out.

Then it was just a matter of time before it consumed the factory farming industry, and nothing was safe. Pigs, chickens, turkeys, cattle, lamb. You name it. If it had flesh, it got infected. Except for cats, dogs, and aquatic life. For some reason, they were spared. The authorities had made it illegal to consume pets, just in case the virus jumped to them. Fish were farmed to near extinction, then protected to the point that the government would rather their people starve to death than overfish their precious sharks. Almost every day the local news reported on fights breaking out on the shores. The National Guard came in, then it all really went to shit. Each person could only be allowed one fish, two crabs, and one miscellaneous item (octopus, etc.) per week. Only adults of each species were allowed, and no females since they could be carrying eggs. For most people, it wasn't worth the trouble. But the cost of grains, wheat, and veggies skyrocketed due to demand, and Carrie and Sam's dad had, along with most of the population, planted their own vegetable gardens in their backyards.

Pets were harder to come by, as most people had taken to eating their own despite the laws against it. Some abandoned their cats and dogs at the shelter to avoid the temptation. They couldn't bring themselves to eat their cat, but a shot of Sodium Pentobarbital to the heart was totally fine. Fluffy could die, but not by their own hands. Bertha had been declared off-limits by Gretchen pretty early on. She reasoned that it didn't make sense to take the cat's entire life for just one meal for the three of them. One meal wouldn't make much of a difference in the long run, anyway, and as long as they had their garden, they didn't *have* to eat her.

"I'm full. Guess my stomach isn't used to this much at one time. Anyway, we need to go pick up Olivia." Carrie leaned back in her chair and sighed. She smiled at Manny. It was good to see him happy for a minute. Fully satiated, and content that her brother would be fine, a nagging thought pulled at the back of her mind. There was something...

"Hey, you need to clean out Bertha's litter box and check for mice. This place fuckin' reeks," Carrie said.

"Agreed." Manny nodded.

"Oh shit, I forgot she was in my room. I didn't want her jumping on the table when I had the food out earlier. I'll let her out when you leave."

"Okay." Another thread tugged at the back of her subconscious, but she couldn't quite put her finger on it.

Carrie and Manny left after making Jason promise to call them if he started feeling worse. They got in their car and pulled out of the driveway when Carrie slammed on the brakes and hit the steering wheel with the palm of her hand.

"That's what bugged me. Where's Dad and Gretchen, if their cars are still here?" She said to Manny.

Carrie pulled the car back onto the driveway.

Manny shrugged, then pulled out his cell phone and dialed Sam's number. "Yo, Jason. Is your dad and Gretchen sick, too?" He listened to Jason talk before continuing, "No, man. Their cars are here. Yeah... Okay... Talk later."

Manny turned to Carrie, her hands still on the wheel and her foot on the brake. "He said they're probably sick also, gonna check on 'em and call us. Let's go home, I'm tired."

Carrie didn't want to leave, but they were already late picking up the baby. The sun rose in the distance as they headed to her mother-in-law's house.

***

Jason hung up the phone and slid further down in his chair. He really *did* feel like shit. He didn't want to admit it to Carrie and Manny; they would have insisted on taking him to Urgent Care and that seemed just way more trouble than he needed. He probably had a stomach bug. At least he still had an appetite. He had just finished off a second dinner and remained famished like he hadn't eaten in years.

Jason placed his palms on the table and pushed himself to a standing position, then headed for the hallway. Carrie was right, it did still stink. Remembering Bertha, he went to his room and opened the door. The cat hissed and ran past him toward the kitchen. The cat door flapped back and forth before settling still.

"Sorry, girl. I forgot." He glanced around his room to see if she had torn anything up but there was only a crumpled receipt she had pulled from the top of the trash can. He couldn't remember throwing anything away, but he shook his head and turned back to the hall. The smell seemed stronger in front of his dad's room. A sick feeling crept into his gut as he reached for the door handle.

Immediately a stench overpowered him, crawling into his nostrils and dripping down into his stomach. He jumped backward and covered his mouth and nose with both hands. Coughing, he bent over and threw up on the carpet in the hall. He stared at the mess as his stomach growled, and he couldn't remember why he stood outside his dad's room.

Jason was famished. He leaned down toward the vomit on the floor but stopped himself just inches from the mess. Partially digested hunks of meat sat atop a yellowish sludge. Jason jumped back in disgust and confusion. He pulled his eyes away from the carpet with every bit of willpower inside him and looked up into his dad's room.

He saw the bed and remembered.

Jason wiped his mouth on his shirt and walked into the bedroom. Resting on top of their recently purchased King-sized memory foam mattress, beneath a thin green blanket, lay the bodies of his dad and stepmom, Gretchen.

Jason had only ever seen one dead body in his entire life, and that had been enough. He had been nine years old at the funeral of his grandmother, his mom's mom. The woman had looked exactly as Jason had always known her, albeit much more quiet than usual. Her eyes had been closed, and her skin glowed with warmth (later he learned that had been thanks to the makeup artist). She had looked *normal*.

That wasn't the case that day in his father's bedroom.

His dad had always been a robust, intimidating man. Standing around 6', 6" with wide shoulders and a former football player turned middle-aged man's build, in life he had been someone to be reckoned with and feared. But in death, his already-light complexion had turned pale, with a wet, greenish tint to it. One of his arms draped across the blanket, and the skin there had turned dark, almost like a bruise, where it rested on the cloth.

The face of the man in front of him was no longer anything to fear. His eyelids sat half-open, and a clear-white substance appeared to have leaked from his mouth and nose.

But the most disgusting, vile part of it all were the small white wriggling things all over his father's corpse. Maggots squirmed in and out of the skin, swimming in the holes they had created.

His stepmom had suffered a similar fate but faced away from Jason toward the wall. He had been spared having to look at the damage death had done to her.

Jason sat on the edge of the bed, shifting the bodies. A fresh wave of stench wafted around the room and the flesh on his dad's face jiggled like a not-quite-fully set pudding. He watched the maggots, mesmerized by their slow dance across the flesh. In, out, up, down, left, right.

As the sun rose in the sky, it threw shafts of light through the windows. The maggots continued their ballet, briefly illuminated by the light as they moved to different sections of his dad's skin. They were beautiful.

****

Carrie stared at the baby monitor as the light flashed red with every whimper from Olivia. She groaned and ignored it, hoping Manny would wake up and get to the baby before she erupted into full-blown cries. But of course, he didn't. Manny was either the world's hardest sleeper, or he pretended so he wouldn't have to get up. Carrie swung her legs onto the floor and stood up, but darkness clouded her vision. She swayed and plopped back down onto the bed. She felt for Manny without looking and swatted the comforter over him.

"Hey. Hey, get up."

Manny moaned, "I don't feel good."

"I don't either, but I think I just blacked out so it's on you." Carrie put her arm across her eyes preemptively to block the light that Manny always turned on when he got up to check on the baby. The bed shifted and a yellow glow shone through a crack between her arm and her face.

Manny grunted and shuffled toward the bedroom door muttering, "You owe me."

"Sure, got it." Carrie kept her eyes covered. Olivia still screamed through the monitor until Manny's voice broke in.

"Hey, peanut. What's this all about, huh? You hungry? Welcome to our world, baby girl." The crib blankets rustled, and Olivia gasped between cries, already exhausted from her ordeal, but she didn't scream again. Manny just had a way with her that Carrie could never understand or replicate. It wasn't fair. She had been the one who had carried the baby for nine months, she's the one who gave birth to her, but Olivia stayed a daddy's girl through and through.

Manny kept cooing to the baby as he changed her diaper, then the monitor went silent as the fridge banged shut and a bottle rattled against the kitchen counter.

Carrie sighed and rolled over, shoving her face into her pillow to block out the light. "Why..." she mumbled into the cotton. Giving up, she turned over again and put her feet on the floor. She waited a minute for the darkness to return, and after a while without anything happening, she stood up and shuffled to the kitchen.

Manny sat at the table, holding Olivia while feeding her the bottle. The baby's eyes were closed but her mouth still worked the nipple. His face glistened with sweat, and he looked pale.

"You okay, babe? You don't look so hot," Carrie said as she poured a glass of water for herself.

"Have *you* looked in a mirror lately?" Manny said. Olivia's eyes fluttered open, then closed again as she kept sucking the bottle.

"If I look anything like I feel, then I know it's rough." Carrie grabbed cold medicine from the cabinet and sat down at the table. She popped a few of the pills and handed the box and glass of water to Manny. "Here, your turn. Let me take her."

"Oh sure, now you get her when she's almost back asleep." Manny smiled and handed the baby to Carrie. Olivia's eyes remained closed. He stood and kissed the top of Carrie's head as he poured his water glass. "Not sharing with you, just in case."

"Clearly we have the same bug, dummy." Carrie rolled her eyes and wiggled the bottle free from Olivia. For a few seconds, her lips stayed pursed, sucking a bottle that wasn't there. She settled back to sleep and Carrie used the sleeve of her shirt to wipe a milk bubble from Olivia's lips.

"I'm starving, want anything?" Manny asked as he pulled soup from the fridge.

"Hell yeah," answered Carrie. "Let me go put her down and I'll be right back."

When Carrie returned, Manny tilted the last of the soup into his mouth.

"Hey! Save some for me," Carrie said, frowning.

Manny set the empty bowl on the table and looked up at his wife, frowning. "Sorry."

Carrie rummaged through the near-empty pantry and produced a stale bag of mini cookies. Once a week the local food bank gave out whatever they had left, usually expired shit. There used to be rules against stuff like that, but that had all gone down the drain along with everything else.

She ate the cookies, then turned back to the cabinet to see what else they had. Manny did the same in the fridge.

***

Jason closed the door to his dad's room and leaned against the wall in the hallway. He couldn't call 911, they'd know what he did and arrest him. No one would care that he didn't mean to kill them, that he didn't know he had given them so many sleeping pills. The truth was, he had killed his dad and stepmom. He looked at the bedroom door and thought he should probably be feeling something, but hunger remained the only thing he knew.

He ate the rest of the cat meat without bothering to cook it first. He wondered why he ever cooked it to start with. Completely raw, it was the most delicious thing he had ever tasted until he ate a pack of crackers from the pantry. Then *that* had been the best thing he had ever eaten. He downed the rest of the crackers, two bags of chips, three apples, and four boxes of raw pasta. When he finished, he lay on the floor of the kitchen, enjoying the feel of the cool tile against his cheek. Bile rose in his throat, and he rolled to the side and puked, not caring that it covered his shirt and jeans. Jason stood up and went to the garage to get more meat from the freezer.

Everything had been frozen solid, so Jason pulled out the rest of the plastic bags and set them on the floor of the garage to let them defrost. He returned to the kitchen and went through the rest of the pantry and the drawers in the fridge. Sometimes his stepmom hid food behind the tofu, knowing he wouldn't touch the stuff.

Jason chuckled. The joke was on her. He had already eaten the tofu *and* the banana pie pudding hiding behind it, all six containers of it.

He threw up again before grabbing his keys and going out the front door. He climbed into his car and headed back to the animal shelter.

From halfway down the street, he could see two black-and-white police cars and an ambulance parked in front of the building. Their sirens were off, but the lights on top of the vehicles flashed, reflecting off the building like sparklers. The cops stood around the ambulance, one talking to a radio on his shoulder, one smoking a cigarette, and a third staring into the back of the ambulance. The hunger within almost had him stop, but there remained enough common sense in Jason to tell him that would be a terrible idea.

He drove on, taking a left on Manor St. before heading south down Wilkins. A blue Chevrolet drove past him, but the windows were tinted so Jason couldn't see the driver. Not many other cars were out, that was one advantage of living in a small town. The nights were nice and quiet. Peaceful.

Ahead, a bright patch of lights from the Wick-Mart gas station and convenience store caught his eye. Jason slowed and pulled into the parking lot. He stared, mesmerized by the seemingly endless rows of canned goods, chips, candy, and other food visible through the large glass windows that covered the front of the building. He smiled, turned the car off, and stepped out onto the pavement.

A woman, probably no older than twenty-one, looked up from her phone when the bell jingled above the front door. Her black hoodie hung on her at least three sizes too large. A boyfriend's perhaps, or maybe she just liked them baggy. A gust of wind blew in around Jason and the silver ring in her septum bounced as she wrinkled her nose.

Jason looked down at the vomit covering his shirt.

"My bad, bro."

He laughed at the clerk and then headed for the food on the shelf closest to him. It was odd, from the parking lot it had seemed like every shelf brimmed with food, but standing in front of them they were all mostly empty. Jason stared at the empty spaces, then back through the large windows to the parking lot and his car. The glass looked normal enough, nothing weird or distorted about it. He shook his head and reached for potato chips, ripped the bag open, and poured them down his throat.

"Yo, dude. You can't do that!" the clerk said as she put her phone down and stood up.

Ignoring her, Jason reached for the only other bag of chips on the shelf, opened them, and ate the entire thing within seconds. When he lowered the bag from his face, the clerk stood right in front of him.

"Dude. What the fuck, man? You gonna pay for that?" She stared at Jason incredulously.

"I don't have any money," Jason said as he turned his back to the clerk, walked past a few more empty spots on the shelf, and stopped in front of a stack of candy bars. He grabbed a handful and shoved them in his pockets before reaching toward a can of tiny canned sausages. Jason pulled the tab on top and opened it. He held the open container over his mouth and poured. Just as the juice hit his throat, the clerk knocked the can from his hands. Jason watched it tumble to the floor, spilling sausages and juice across the aisle.

"Why..." Jason said as he looked up at the clerk, confused.

He knelt and picked up the sausages from the floor, popping them into his mouth before the clerk could swat those away as well. Jason stood and walked to the next aisle, looking for more food.

"Dude, *gross*," the clerk said as she hurried to catch up with Jason.

He held his stomach as it turned and twisted. Bile rose into his throat and he puked onto the empty shelf in front of him. He wiped his mouth and looked down at his hands. A chunk of sausage perched on the back of his left hand atop a smear of half-digested chips and stomach fluids. He licked the meat from his skin and walked toward the chilled section on the back wall of the store.

Behind him, the clerk also threw up after seeing what Jason had just eaten. He looked over his shoulder at the pool on the floor, mingling with his own. Jason dropped to his knees and scooped the liquid and unidentifiable chunks into his mouth with both hands. The clerk grabbed his shoulder and Jason pushed her away with his elbows, trying not to spill the vomit he had been scooping up.

"Dude," the clerk yelled as she grabbed Jason's arm.

Jason picked up the empty can of sausages from the floor and spun around, swinging it toward the clerk. The pull-tab metal top was still attached, and it left a streak of blood across her face as he swung. She touched the wound and stared at Jason without speaking or blinking. She backed up and tripped in the vomit on the floor, hitting her shoulder against the edge of the metal shelf on the way down.

Jason watched her fall and looked down at the can still in his hand. He stood and shuffled to where she lay on the floor, his feet slick against the wet tile. She mumbled, holding her shoulder with one hand and the scratch on her face with the other.

Her eyes met his and she screamed, "Don't hurt me. I won't say nothin'. Just go...*please.*"

Jason tilted his head to the side, then looked at the food still on the shelves. He needed to eat in peace, she kept trying to make him stop eating. He turned back to her and brought the can down on her forehead. She yelled out in surprise and pain, and he raised it and pounded it back down onto her nose. Blood spurted on his shirt and face as he continued hitting her with the can until she stopped making noises.

Jason turned back to the floor and continued eating.

***

Carrie lay next to a man on the kitchen floor in a pool of vomit, staring at the open refrigerator. They had emptied the majority of the food hours before. All that remained were a few cans of baby formula. From their position, the fridge light behind the formula glowed, creating soft, bright edges around the can. Carrie stared, wondering why they were still there. She vaguely remembered telling the man they couldn't eat it, but at that moment she didn't have a single reason not to. She stood up, grabbed one of the cans, and shoved her finger under the pull tab, breaking the seal open with a satisfying click.

"Give me that," the man said as he stood and fumbled toward the formula in her hand.

The can slipped out of her hand and crashed to the floor, spilling formula across the white tile. Carrie stared down at the mess, then up at the strange man. Frowning, she turned and reached for the other can still on the shelf in the fridge. He also tried to grab that one, but she moved it out of his way before he could take it from her. He grunted and pushed her against the kitchen counter, knocking the can from her hand. It clattered onto the floor and rolled away from them.

Carrie grabbed a knife from the block by the stove, pulling it from its slot with a metallic swish. She plunged it into the man's stomach, twisting it as she pushed. He stared up at her, his mouth gaping open in confusion. She pulled the knife out and stuck it into the side of his neck. It slid in like a hot knife in a tub of butter. Carrie always loved butter and put it on everything she could. He tried to scream but only a gurgle came out as he fell. Blood spurted onto the floor creating a thick pinkish sludge where it mixed with the formula and vomit.

She walked to the other end of the kitchen, picked up the can, and opened it. As she drank, a baby cried from the other end of the house. Carrie wiped the drops of formula off her mouth with the back of her hand and stared at the off-white smear across her skin. She headed toward the crying noise, licking her hand as she went.

At the far end of the hallway, a door opened into a room. Light from inside poured into the hallway in a narrow slice, illuminating the tan carpet. Inside the room, a screaming baby lay in a crib. The red-faced baby had rolled against one of the hot pink crib bumpers and gotten stuck. Urine soaked the bottom half of its body and the swollen diaper had expanded past the edges of a yellow onesie. A white letter "O" had been embroidered on the front of the clothing and Carrie wondered what it stood for. Beneath the baby lay a white and pink striped sheet, dark and damp. The infant had spit up, and Carrie stared at the yellow froth on the baby's chin. She picked up the baby and leaned forward, sniffing its face. Carrie licked the formula off the baby's mouth, and held it up, staring at the bright blue eyes wet with tears. Carrie's hands, wet with urine, slipped and she lost her grip on the baby. The child tumbled to the floor, knocking its head against the leg of a rocking chair before settling into a quiet heap at Carrie's feet. She stared at the baby, tilted her head as if trying to remember something, then left the room to look for more food.

***

Jason ran through the alley behind Wick-Mart, sniffing the air around him frantically. He tripped on a crack in the concrete and fell into a pile of trash bags next to a dumpster. Blood seeped from a hole in his jeans over his knee, but nothing hurt. He remembered blood *should* hurt but didn't know why.

A loud, piercing wail echoed through the alley. The screech ebbed and flowed like the tide. Jason never did like to surf.

Delicious scents seeped into the air from the big metal square in front of him. He couldn't figure out how to get to what lay inside and crawled around it, crying. Blood from his hands left smears across the dumpster as he circled. He couldn't remember why the dumpster had bloody handprints on it. Or why there was also blood on his pants and shirt.

"Hey!"

Jason peeked around the corner of the dumpster. A tall blue man stood in front of the open rear door of the store. He held a gray box out to Jason and told him to get down on his knees. Jason looked down at the blood on his knee but didn't want to make a mess, so he stood and walked toward the man.

A shot rang out from the gray box and a sharp pain drilled into Jason's right arm.

"Owww," he cried as he jumped back behind the dumpster and held his left hand over the wound. That didn't seem fair.

The man yelled at him again, closer and louder than he had been before.

Jason sprinted away from the store, driven by some distant, unconscious urge to get to the animal shelter. Behind him, more noises rang out into the night. He wasn't sure why the gray box kept trying to bite him, but he ran until he couldn't hear the sounds anymore. A few blocks away, Jason passed a group of teenagers smoking in the parking lot of an abandoned store.

"Yo, what's the rush?" they yelled out to him as he passed.

He heard what they were saying, but the words held no meaning as he continued down the road.

Jason stopped once he arrived in the empty parking lot of the animal shelter and put his hands on his knees as he fought to catch his breath. His head weighed a hundred pounds and lights flashed across his eyes before he fell to the ground, exhausted. Bile rose in the back of his throat, but he swallowed it back down, chewing the larger chunks, and stood. He looked at the street, but the blue man and gray box were no longer behind him. He walked to the back of the building.

A red brick sat near the closed door, and he wondered what it all meant. He turned the handle, but the door didn't budge. A window sat in the middle of the door, narrow and tall just about at eye level. Jason picked up the brick and banged it into the glass. It broke, sending sharp pieces flying into the building, and barking erupted from within. He dropped the brick and reached through the opening, feeling around until he located the door handle and unlocked it. As he withdrew his arm, bits of glass still stuck to the frame cut into his skin. He stared at the blood welling up and the flesh hanging in spots.

Jason opened the door and entered the animal shelter.

***

Carrie sat in the kitchen in a pool of spilled baby formula, leftover vegetable soup, and her vomit, wondering where she could find more food. She leaned against a man's dead body, picked up his hand, and held it in hers. There had been something there, once. Something good and pure.

The front door jiggled and opened a few inches before the chain latch caught it.

"Carrie! Manny! Open the door!" an older woman screamed.

Carrie pulled herself up and walked into the living room toward the noise.

She stared at the latch, pulled taut between the door and the frame. Peeking through the gap were flashes of gray and red.

"Carrie! Open the door and let me in!"

She shut the door and touched the chain, unsure how to do what the woman wanted her to do. After a few fumbling tries, she succeeded in removing the latch and the door opened.

The woman rushed into the room, eyes frantic and searching. "Where's Manny? Where's Olivia? Are you guys okay?"

Carrie stared at the other woman's short gray hair and how it contrasted with her bright red shirt collar.

"Carrie?" The woman turned to look at her for the first time. "Oh my god, are you okay? What happened?"

Carrie's eyes were glued to the shirt collar, then the brown skin next to it, and how it jiggled as the woman spoke.

The woman grabbed Carrie's shoulders and shook her. "Look at me! Where are Manny and Olivia!?"

Carrie laughed. The woman's throat continued to wiggle and the shirt color jumped up and down with each word.

She dropped Carrie's shoulders in disgust and looked at her hands. Something strange covered them, but Carrie didn't care. The woman wiped her hands on her jeans and walked into the kitchen.

"Nooooooooooooooooo," she wailed. Her scream was beautiful, from a deep, dark place. It danced before Carrie in shades of red.

"The baby!" The woman ran from the kitchen to a room at the end of the hallway where she screamed again, the sound muffled by something. "Come on, come on, wake up!"

Carrie frowned. Her hunger returned, banishing the dance of red in her living room. She shuffled through the open door and down her driveway. As she stepped onto the street, a baby cried.

She stopped and turned toward the house. A palpation of memory hung in her head, but she couldn't figure out what it dangled from or how it swayed. Carrie stared at the house with one corner of her mouth turned down as a truck slammed into her.

***

Jason left the door open behind him as he walked down the corridor. Snarls and yips continued to ooze from a room off to his right. He stopped in front of the room and peeked in, curious to see if the noises were coming from someone who had anything to eat.

But there was no food, just rows and rows of metal boxes containing loud, furry things. Sharp teeth and mean eyes bore into him as he stepped into the room. In the corner, a tiny fuzzy ball whimpered.

He went to it and knelt, reaching out his hand. It stepped forward, sniffed him, and recoiled back into the corner. Frowning, Jason stood and left the room.

He took a few steps into the hall before collapsing in a fit of coughs. He fell to his hands and knees onto the chipped linoleum floor. Blood dripped onto the floor in front of him. He wiped his mouth and when he pulled his hand back, a smear of blood had streaked across his skin. Beneath the blood, a circle of exposed flesh tingled. He wiped his hand on his shirt and stared at it again. Thick, yellow pus seeped from the wound.

His legs also burned, and when he pulled his jeans up past his calves, similar craters of raw flesh cried the same yellow ooze.

Jason rolled onto his back and stared at the ceiling. Swirls of white and gray crashed like waves on the stained tiles above him. Something wet touched his cheek and whimpered. He didn't know what it could be, but it felt soft and good. The thing moved toward his leg, sniffing. His jeans were still pulled up, exposing his calf and the wounds quickly spreading across it. Jason registered a faint tugging as the thing pulled on the exposed, raw flesh. It ripped pieces of his leg and growled while it ate.

Jason smiled as everything went black.

-Acknowledgements-

I'm eternally grateful to all the publishers who took a chance on me in the beginning and those who continue to do so. Special thanks to *The Bookends Review* for your acceptance of "Flap". It was my first time to get a congratulatory email and while it wasn't my first published piece due to publishing schedules, I'll never forget that feeling of acceptance. You made it all so easy and fun. The amazing folks over at *The Sirens Call* were the first to put my words into the world with "The Dinner Rush" and a poem titled "Let You Go". We've continued to work together since then, and I can't say enough about the fantastic stuff you guys create. Thank you also to *Rue Scribe*, Claire Buss, the *Australian Writers' Centre*, Stuart Conover, Stephanie Ellis, *Emerge Literary Journal*, Mark Bilsborough, the *Women on Writing* crew, *Stanchion* Magazine, Jennifer Bernardini, Janine Pipe and Jill Gerardi, *Pontoon* Magazine, Red Lagoe, Elaine Pascale, and Megan Cannella. Thank you to all of the beta readers through the years who have read and given feedback on almost every story in this collection. Thank you to the incredible cover artist Lynne Hansen. Seeing this pre-made cover inspired me to put this collection together and you've been an absolute delight to work with. Thank you to my amazing family for your endless and unconditional support. Thank you to my annoying dogs who love to lay behind my desk chair so I can't move, forcing me to sit and write when I really need to use the bathroom or get a drink. And thank you, reader, if you've gotten this far. Not everyone reads these things, but I see you and I appreciate you.

-Previously Published-

"**Regulators**." Short Story. *Generation X-Ed* Anthology, 325-353. Dark Ink Books, 2022.

"**Flap**." Flash Fiction. *The Bookends Review*. July 5, 2019. http://thebookendsreview.com/.

"**Flap**." Flash Fiction. *Isolation* Anthology, Fantasia Divinity, 2019.

"**Blood of the Rougarou**." Short Story. *Dancing in the Shadows: A Tribute to Anne Rice* Anthology, 55-65. Yuriko Publishing, 2022.

"**Blood of the Rougarou**." Chapbook. "Wintertide Feast" Custom Box, Persephone Light Co, 2021.

"**Even the Jellyfish**." Flash Fiction. Finalist, Winter 2021 Flash Fiction Contest, Women on Writing, May 2021. https://wow-womenonwriting.com

"**Even the Jellyfish**." Flash Fiction. *Emerge Literary Journal no. 17*, February 2021. https://emergeliteraryjournal.com

"**Step Right Up**." Short Story. *Pontoon vol. 1*, 69-76. Malarkey Books, Spring 2022.

"**How to Pose the Dead**." Short Story. *Slash-Her: An Anthology of Women in Horror*, 28-44. Kandisha Press, 2022.

"**Trash Bags.**" Poem. *The Siren's Call no. 59*, 143, October 2022. http://www.sirenscallpublications.com

"**Those Goddamn Strawberries.**" Short Story. *Next Week On... A Reality TV Anthology*, 7-9. On Tap Publishing, 2023.

"**Her Mother's Smile.**" Flash Fiction. *Trembling With Fear: Year 4*, 43-44. The Horror Tree, 2021.

"**Her Mother's Smile.**" Flash Fiction. *Trembling With Fear*, The Horror Tree, February 9, 2020. https://horrortree.com

"**Two Months Too Long.**" Short Story. *Found: An Anthology of Found Footage Horror Stories*, 3-26. Vermillion 2 One, 2022.

"**Fire in the Night**." Flash Fiction. *The Siren's Call no. 46*, 30, August 2019. http://www.sirenscallpublications.com

"**Liberty Bell.**" Flash Fiction. *Trembling With Fear*, The Horror Tree, February 14, 2020. https://horrortree.com

"**Liberty Bell.**" Flash Fiction. *Trembling With Fear: More Tales From the Tree: Vol. 3*, 21-22. The Horror Tree, 2021.

"**Flesh Communion.**" Short Story. *American Cannibal* Anthology, 321-335. Maenad Press, 2023.

"**A Werewolf's Lament.**" Flash Fiction. *Wyldblood Press.* February 12, 2021. https://wyldblood.com

"**A Werewolf's Lament.**" Flash Fiction. *The Call of the Wyld (Wyldblood Anthologies)*, 27-28. Wyldblood Press, 2021.

"**The Bay Sirius Witch of Atchafalaya Basin**." Short Story. *Pen to Print*, Write On Showcase, October 16, 2019. https://pentoprint.org

"**The Bay Sirius Witch of Atchafalaya Basin.**" Short Story. *Haunted* Anthology, 65-66. CB Visions, 2019.

"**I Watch Them**." Flash Fiction. Short-Listed, Furious Fiction Contest, Australian Writers' Centre. December 23, 2019. https://www.writerscentre.com.au

"**The Finest French Lace**." Flash Fiction. *The Siren's Call no. 59*, 22-23, October 2022. http://www.sirenscallpublications.com

"**Just a Dream**." Short Story. *The Nightmare Never Ends: An Anthology of Horror*, 149-160. Exploding Head Fiction, 2023.

"**The Many Indiscretions of Agent 592**." Short Story. *Nightside: Tales of Outre Noir*, 1-5. Close to the Bone Publishing. 2020

"**Three Acts**." Flash Fiction. *Stanchion, no. 5*, 35-36, August 2021.

"**The Dinner Rush**." Short Story. *The Siren's Call no. 44*, 22-23, April 2019. http://www.sirenscallpublications.com

"**When the Swell Breaks**." Flash Fiction. *Rue Scribe*, Underwood Press. August 15, 2019. https://underwoodpress.com/ruescribe/

"**Star of San Luis**." Short Story. *Nightmare Sky: Stories of Astronomical Horror* Anthology, 223-234. Death Knell Press, 2022.

"**Cat Food**." Novelette. *Table for 3: A Charity Anthology*, 87-166. Easton Falls Publishing, 2023.

-About the Author-

Holly Rae Garcia works full-time as the Gulf Coast Regional Photographer for a global chemical company. Growing up, she read her mother's extensive Stephen King and True Crime collection, and a love for dark fiction with sad endings has stayed with her ever since. Holly especially loves the works of Edgar Allen Poe, Daniel Keyes, Richard Matheson, Stephen King, and Alfred Hitchcock.

Her own books include *Parachute, Come Join the Murder,* and *The Easton Falls Massacre: Bigfoot's Revenge* (co-written with her husband and fellow author, Ryan Prentice Garcia). Her shorter fiction has been published online and in print for various magazines and anthologies. Holly is a member of the Horror Writers Association and the Alliance of Independent Writers.

She lives on the Texas Coast with her family. You can often find her reading, watching horror movies, or playing poker.

www.HollyRaeGarcia.com

-Also By Holly Rae Garcia-

"AL-13N FLU: A Short Horror Story"

Parachute

Come Join the Murder

The Easton Falls Massacre: Bigfoot's Revenge

9 798989 513918